Hamad M.

Christiana Elfwood is the pseudonym of Christiane Sourvinou-Inwood, a classical scholar who was born in Greece.

She has taught Classics and Classical Archaeology at the Universities of Liverpool, Reading and Oxford, and published six books and many articles on Greek religion, mythology, tragedy, comedy, archaeology, and ancient perceptions of women and death – including studies of the sanctuary and cult of Artemis at Brauron (near Athens): the setting for *Murder Most Classical*.

MURDER MOST CLASSICAL

CHRISTIANA ELFWOOD

MURDER MOST CLASSICAL

Vanguard Press

VANGUARD PAPERBACK

© Copyright 2007
Christiana Elfwood

A CIP catalogue record for this title is
available from the British Library.

ISBN 978 1 84386 357 1

Vanguard Press is an imprint of
Pegasus Elliot MacKenzie Publishers Ltd.

www.pegasuspublishers.com

First Published in 2007

Vanguard Press
Sheraton House Castle Park
Cambridge England

Printed & Bound in Great Britain

Chapter One

They think I should be grateful. After all, where would I be without them? They took care of me – as they put it – when my father fled the country and died, after he was convicted of treason, and all his property was sold off, and the man I was about to marry said the situation had now changed and he couldn't marry me. I wouldn't be here now if it hadn't been for them, I know. And yes, I am happy here. But grateful? It makes me boil up inside when I think that they expect me to be grateful. They say 'what made you think life is supposed to be fair?', but it's a different story if *they* don't get what they want, what they believe is their due. I try not to dwell on things, I really do like it here, but sometimes it all comes flooding back, and the bile bursts into my mouth and I have to swallow it before I can go and do my job.

Chapter Two

When the war between Athens and Sparta was over, and the peace treaty was signed, Mego, the priestess of Artemis Orthia at Sparta, decided to visit Athens. Her son had been killed in the last days of the fighting, and she thought that maybe going to Athens, visiting the goddess' sanctuaries in Athens, might help – if anything could, but then… 'Don't think like that' she told herself. 'Don't think. Just look at the view.'

She was on her way to the sanctuary of Artemis Brauronia, on the East coast of Attica, a long way outside the city. As the carriage came down the hill on the last lap of the road from Athens she saw a green valley between hills that went all the way down into the sea. The brutal midday light seared razor sharp outlines into the intensely blue flats of the sky and the sea. Everything was limpid clarity. She could see the sanctuary among the vineyards and the fig orchards, one end climbing up the lower slope of a hill, its buildings shining in the sun, some strongly coloured, others blinding white in their unpainted marble. There was a small palm grove, and a placid little river snaked its way through. Mego knew that this was an important sanctuary, but she hadn't come to see its fine buildings and the rich dedications, she wanted to observe the little bears, and, of course, see the festival itself, which only took place every fifth year.

At last the carriage reached the sanctuary's gatehouse and Mego got out. An attractive dark-haired woman in her early thirties had been sitting on the bench, clearly waiting for Mego, for she now came forward, welcomed Mego and introduced herself. She was Chloe, the subpriestess of Artemis Brauronia.

Chloe escorted Mego to her guest quarters, left her there for a short time to wash and freshen up, and generally recover from the journey, and then she took her to meet the priestess, Theano. Theano was probably a few years younger that Mego herself, and some years older than Chloe. Early forties, Mego guessed. Her hair was still blond, and she was tall and statuesque and very elegant. Mego had been assuming that Theano would show her around the sanctuary, give her a guided tour, tell her how it worked and how it was run, and compare notes. But in fact it soon became clear that this was to be a brief meeting, and that it was Chloe who was going to be Mego's guide and hostess, not the priestess herself. Chloe seemed to be a warmer person than Theano, at least on the surface, but Mego was irritated that Theano felt that she was too grand to bother with Mego personally – or that Mego wasn't grand enough. 'Who does she think she is?' she told herself. 'The cult of Artemis Orthia is a more important cult in Sparta than that of Artemis Brauronia is in Athens.' Then she realized that she had been obsessing about trivialities – even if only for a short fraction of time – and she was glad.

Chloe knew what was in Mego's mind – or so she thought – and she was tempted to say nothing, but then she decided that she ought to explain. "It's not what you think, Mego," she said. "It's not that Theano can't be bothered to show you around. It's just that I do most of the actual running of the sanctuary, and of the school, and there is no point in you getting it all second-hand. This is what we always do."

"Why is that?"

"What do you mean?

"Why isn't the priestess running things?"

"Well, as you may have gathered, this sanctuary, and especially the school, are very important for the city." She hesitated.

"And?" Mego prompted her.

"And, I don't know what things are like in Sparta, but here priestesses are not appointed for what they can do, but for who their families are. That's the truth, whatever they may say; it's dressed up in different ways in different cases, with elections or appointment by lot, or whatever, but the reality is that since it is not possible to have a man do the job, they make sure that they appoint the right sort of woman. My family is not what you would call a 'good' family, and in any case I am not the right sort of woman; and Theano is very good at weaving."

"Weaving?"

"Yes, we have to teach the girls weaving; of course their mothers can do it just as well, and in fact do, but they feel it is important to have us teach them as well, to signpost our aims of preparing the girls to be good wives and mothers; and Theano is very good at it."

Mego laughed. "That's a very strange reason for choosing a priestess."

"That's not the real reason, that's what I am saying, the real reason is that she comes from the right family and she has the right sort of personality. And she and her rich friends bring in money and gifts."

"I can see this is a rich sanctuary."

"Yes, we are doing fine, in fact we are doing much better than most, even in these difficult times, because of the school. Old pupils make donations all the time."

"Tell me about the school. I told you, this is really what I came to see. I want to understand exactly how it's different from ours in Sparta."

"Well, obviously, it's not really a school, not like the schools boys go to; we just call it that unofficially. It's a religious service for the goddess. Forty girls between the ages of five and ten come and live in the sanctuary for a year. During this year they are called 'bears', and they dance and sing for the goddess, which we teach them to do, and we teach them to read and write and a few other things, like weaving. They do gymnastics and they swim in the sea, and run races and they hunt."

"I am very surprised to hear all this, I must say. I thought girls weren't allowed to do that sort of thing in Athens. One hears that you Athenians think that we Spartans are depraved, because our girls get what you call a masculine education."

Chloe laughed. "Well, some of what you heard is men's wish-fulfilment; they like to pretend that here women are under their total control, which is good, while you let girls do all sorts of things, which is bad. I think the differences are less dramatic, but it's true that our girls don't have the same freedom as yours. And, of course, what we do here at Brauron is not for everyone, and it doesn't last long, but it does happen; you do get all these experiences if you are chosen to be a bear. Obviously, only girls from the best families are chosen, though they are supposed to do it on behalf of all the girls who were born in the same year. Anyway, these chosen girls have to come and be bears to propitiate the goddess because someone a long time ago had killed a tame bear around these parts. At the end of their year here there is a sort of graduating ceremony, at the festival, which you'll see for yourself, and then they are ready for marriage."

Mego was appalled. "Not at six surely! I never heard of such a thing! I know you think we get married late in Sparta, but this is ridiculous...! I don't believe it!"

"No, no... They don't get married then; they are simply

ready to become marriageable; we turn them into civilized young ladies before they have their first period. That's why they can't be older than ten. It has to be done before their first period, however early this may be. Usually they don't get married before they are fourteen, and most people think that the right age is around sixteen."

"Right. I see..." Mego wasn't sure if she had given offence with her reaction, so she struggled to find something to say that might create a rapport. Eventually she asked "What about you? Are you married?"

"No, I'm not married," Chloe said. "Are you?"

"Yes, I've been married for many years. My children are grown up. I have one son and one daughter." Mego paused and then went on, "I had one son and one daughter. My son was killed in the last days of the war. He was twenty-two." She hadn't meant to say that. She had meant to act as though it hadn't happened, for as long as she could at any one time. After all, the people here didn't need to know, and it would only cause embarrassment. As it evidently did now.

Chloe was visibly horrified; she didn't know how to respond, so she said the only thing she could say. "Oh no... I'm so very sorry."

Mego knew that she needed to make clear that she hadn't meant to imply any blame, that she wasn't even thinking 'You Athenians killed my son, maybe your brother, or your father killed my son.' So she told Chloe something of what she felt as a token of this. "You know, you mustn't believe all you hear about Spartan mothers, that we'd rather have our sons killed than dishonoured in battle, and that we all tell them to die rather than run away. It's..." she stopped, and then went on "It's difficult to explain. We do, of course believe that our men have to fight and die for our country. But losing a son, it's like you are not quite alive any more, and yet you are, and you have to carry on being alive and doing all the things you are supposed to be doing. You don't want to, but you've got to, what else can you do? If you don't there's nothing but a dark abyss."

"I am so sorry. I can't imagine what it must be like." Chloe paused. "Actually, personally, I am not at all sure that I do believe that men have to fight and die for their country. I think it should depend on what the war is for. If it's truly to save our city from tyranny and barbarism, yes, I agree, but how often is this true? And how often foolish men have convinced themselves and others that going to war is a good idea?"

"You think that this war between our cities was one of those times?"

"Of course I do. Don't you?"

"I don't want to think that my son died for nothing."

"He didn't die for nothing." Chloe stated emphatically. "He died for his country. Whether what his country was doing at the time was right or wrong doesn't change that."

Mego closed her eyes for what seemed like a second, and then touched Chloe's arm. "If only it were you and me who made the decisions..." she said, and paused, then went on, more hesitantly, "That's one reason why I came. I wanted to make some sort of contact..." She paused again, then went on in a different voice. "To go back to what we were saying, I would very much like to see what you teach the little bears. I realize that you are at the end of the course now, and it's probably a very tense time for them, just before the festival, but I'd like to see what I can."

"As I said, you are very welcome, but I'm warning you, don't expect anything revolutionary by your standards."

Chloe led Mego past a small stone bridge over the quiet stream towards a group of little girls dressed in short saffron yellow robes. There were about forty girls waiting under the palm trees, some looking as young as six, other as old as ten. Some of the girls were running on the spot as though warming up, others were jumping up and down, and some were pushing and shoving each other. Four older girls were shouting at this last group without getting any observable response.

"Those four girls," Mego said, "they look much older than the others; what are they, fourteen? sixteen? Who are they?"

"They are old pupils, former bears who come and help with the little girls when they first arrive, and again in the last month before the festival. It's an extra honour, on top of being a bear, to be selected to come back and help. Of course only the daughters of the very very best families qualify to be selected."

They came up to the group and Chloe introduced the four older girls to Mego. She told her their names, but Mego only took in the one, Daphne, because the girl was stunningly beautiful. She was as tall and golden-haired and perfect as a picture of Artemis hunting in the woods with her companions – though she didn't seem to have the authority to match, not with the little bears at least. They were baiting her and she didn't know how to handle it.

"That's enough." Chloe's voice made the unruly group ripple and go still. All the little girls gathered around her. Chloe looked at them sternly, turning round to make all of them think that she was staring at each individually. "Obviously, I don't want you to panic. However …there are only a few days left before the festival. Now, I am not saying that things arc bad. Your choruses are fine, so I am not worried about the hymns. But you have got to pull yourselves together for the dances; you are supposed to be graceful young ladies now, not wild colts kicking around in a field. Especially in the dance just before you take your clothes off. Let's have another rehearsal of that."

The little girls formed into four groups according to age; they put wreaths of flowers on their heads, from the baskets Daphne and the other three had brought over, and then they danced around a large stone that did duty for the altar of the goddess – which obviously they weren't allowed to use for practice. Eventually, they took off their clothes in front of the 'altar', one by one, threw them into a heap, ran round the altar, and then stood in line, naked, waiting to run a race. Chloe explained. "This is the climax. They shed the saffron robe they are wearing while they are bears, they run the race naked, and eventually they come back to parade and dance and sing in new grown-up clothes as finished young ladies, ready to start on the ladder to becoming Athenian wives and mothers, and wearing golden bees as ornaments."

"Because the bee symbolizes the ideal wife," Mego added.

"Exactly."

The basic mentality behind it wasn't very different from the ceremonies known to Mego that involved acculturating the wild girl children, turning them into civilized young ladies suitable for becoming citizen wives and mothers. It's just that normally the girls would be older, and they would be ready for marriage straight away.

The little girls had lined up for the race. Chloe gave a command and they started running. The four older girls approached the women.

"How do you like our sanctuary, then?" Daphne asked Mego. "Is it like the ones you've got at Sparta?"

"I find it very interesting. A very interesting experience altogether. I am looking forward to seeing more, especially the festival."

"Oh, yes, that really is fantastic," said one of the other girls – whose name Mego eventually found out was Electra –

bubbling with enthusiasm. "I think it was the greatest day of my life, when I was a bear at the festival, a few years ago."

Daphne laughed. "That's pathetic," she said. "That nothing more exciting has ever happened to you than being a bear at the festival. When are you going to get a life?"

"Shut up Daphne," one of the other two older girls cut in. "We've had it up to here with your yapping, on and on all the time."

As the runners came round from behind the palm trees Mego could see a slim dark-haired girl of about ten running breast to breast – or what would have been breast to breast, if either had any – with a sturdy rather squarefaced child with frizzyish fair hair of about the same age.

"Here they are. It's Kallisto and Melissa at the front, as usual," Electra said. "Kallisto is the one with the dark hair," she explained to Mego.

Suddenly the dark-haired girl stumbled and fell, and the fair-haired one went on to win the race. She jumped up and down yelling, but the other girl came up to Chloe shouting "She tripped me."

"That's a lie. She's just a sore loser. I didn't trip her; she should watch where she's going, she's always clumsy."

"You did trip me, and it's not fair." Kallisto was now crying, though she was trying hard not to. Melissa laughed and skipped away.

Electra went up to Kallisto and hugged her. "Come on, now. Don't cry. Don't let that spoiled brat upset you."

"I'll tell Theano you called her niece a spoiled brat." Daphne's shrill voice cut in. "You know you aren't supposed to take sides, you are supposed to be neutral. But of course we all know why you break the rules. Because you fancy Kallisto's brother."

18

"I do not." Electra squealed, burning red with embarrassment and trying to avoid Kallisto's eyes, which had turned towards her, surprise and curiosity drying their tears. One of the other two girls (Anthea, as it subsequently turned out) noticed what was going on, and told Kallisto to run along, which, very reluctantly, she did. Electra regained some sort of control, and said to Daphne "You think everyone is like you, obsessing about men all the time."

"If you aren't thinking about men it's only because men aren't thinking about you." Daphne retorted with a smile. "You would if they did, but who could possibly fancy you?" She looked Electra up and down, slowly moving her eyes from the other girl's face to her body, and back again, and then she shook her head and smiled.

In reality Electra was attractive, curvaceous and well proportioned – all four helpers were good looking. However, Mego knew, many young women believe the worst of their appearance, and, of course, anyone would feel plain when compared to Daphne. Indeed, Electra's body language showed that the taunts had hit their target. But Daphne went on.

"Just as well, really, that you've got to marry your father's brother when your father dies, which can't be too long now. Even a disgusting old man must be better than nothing."

"That's a lie, you are a horrible liar. I don't have to marry my father's brother and my father isn't going to die. He's much better now." Electra's voice cracked and her eyes filled up. She bit her lips but she couldn't stop. She put her head down and ran away towards the small artificial lake beyond the palm trees. Daphne laughed and went to sit under a tree not far from the others.

"Don't worry, I'll make sure Electra is all right," Anthea said to Mego, who had looked rather disturbed at this dramatic development, especially as she was the only adult present – Chloe had gone over to the bears to give them her comments on the race. "I'll go to her in a minute. She will be mortified to have made an exhibition of herself in front of you, but you saw Daphne; she always knows how to find your weakest spot and dig the pins in."

"What was that about?" Mego asked Anthea, "I'm afraid I missed the point."

Chloe, who was now back, also wanted to know what had happened. "Daphne was teasing Electra about being an epikleros again ...well not teasing really, tormenting more like, and Electra got very upset," Anthea answered her, and then went on to repeat what Daphne had said about Kallisto's brother.

Mego was still mystified. "I don't understand," she said. "What's an epikleros, and why does Electra have to marry her father's brother when her father dies? Or does she?"

"Ah well, I'll explain," Chloe said, nodding to Anthea who left to go and bring Electra back. The fourth girl, whose name – it eventually emerged – was Helena, followed her. "It's not in fact quite as bad as it will sound to you. The theory is worse than the practice, truly. What it is, is, if a girl has no brothers, and if her father hasn't adopted a son, which they often do, she becomes the heiress to her father's estate; and to keep the money in the family, when her father dies her paternal male relatives can claim her in marriage in a certain order, first her father's brother, then the father's brother's son, and so on... In theory they can do that even if she is married, they can break up her marriage, unless she already has sons; but in practice this hasn't happened for ...oh, I don't know ...a very long time; the court wouldn't do it, I don't think, not in this day and age, if they ever did."

"But that's dreadful!" Mego interrupted her. "It's barbaric! I

20

can't believe that it happens in Athens, which prides itself on being so civilized..." 'There I go again', she thought as soon as she had said it. 'Criticizing and giving offence at every turn. And it's not as though Chloe approves of the practice; she's obviously very uncomfortable about it. Well, any woman would be.'

"As I said," Chloe was responding in the meantime, "it hasn't happened for a very long time. And some girls are probably happy to be claimed, especially if they are not very attractive, or if they are in love with the cousins who may claim them. It's true though that for many it is a threat hanging over their head, especially when their father is very rich, like Electra's is."

Mego's indignation swamped her good intentions. "And we think things are tough in Sparta. To force a woman to leave her husband; a girl to marry her father's brother."

"It's more likely to be her father's brother's son, but, as I said, it's not very likely it will happen; only, of course, you never know. Legally, girls like Electra are totally vulnerable."

"Can't anything be done?"

"Well, yes, in general, but not in Electra's case, I think. There is one way the father of an epikleros can let his daughter marry the man she wants and protect the marriage; he can adopt her chosen husband. But if it's true what Daphne said about Electra being in love with Kallisto's brother Kallias, that's not an option in this case. Even if he loves her – and we don't know that he does – he wouldn't want to be adopted out of his family. It's an important family, and he doesn't need the money. And his father would certainly have something to say about that idea. I suppose, if Daphne's right, that's why Electra is so sensitive about the whole thing. And her father is not in the best of health – at least he wasn't when her grandmother brought her to the sanctuary about a month ago. Daphne really is a beastly little..."

21

She stopped.

"Not one of your favourite pupils, then," Mego commented, just as she saw Anthea and Helena returning with Electra. Daphne rose from under the tree and smiled serenely in their direction. As soon as she was within shouting distance Electra blurted out what was obviously a rehearsed speech that didn't come out quite right.

"You know something, Daphne, I think it's better not to have a brother and be an epikleros, than to have a brother like yours who hates you, because your father left his mother to marry your mother; and then he died and you've got to do what your brother tells you."

Daphne continued to smile. "Did you think this up all by yourself, then, or did your little friends help you?"

"Stop this childish bickering and go and look after the bears," Chloe ordered the four girls, and they all obeyed immediately, even Daphne, Mego was interested to see.

"Cruel, but true," Chloe said to Mego when they had gone. "What Electra said, I mean. Daphne's brother thinks that that's what killed his mother, his father leaving her. And I must say, Daphne's mother is one of the most devious and manipulative people I have ever met – which is saying something in this job. Like in yours, I imagine. Now their father is dead, the brother is doing his duty by her, anything else wouldn't suit his image, and I am sure that he'll give a very good dowry. But he cannnot stand the sight of her. Their younger brother he doesn't seem to mind quite so much; his hatred had probably been spent out by the time he was born."

"Poor Daphne!"

"I wouldn't waste your sympathy. She's apparently very much admired by the young men, not surprisingly, and she could have her pick of a husband. And she's not exactly deprived of love, you know. She's the apple of her mother's eye, and the darling of her mother's circle. And her younger brother is her slave. I would say that she's had too much love and attention, if anything. Unfortunately, her half-brother is here at the moment, staying at the sanctuary; he is one of the overseers of the sacred rites, the public officials responsible for the administration of the festival, and he has been ignoring her whenever he could ever since he arrived. That probably explains why she's been behaving like this; usually her claws are well sheathed and elegantly wielded."

"You are saying that it's her pride that is hurt."

"Yes, that, but also... Look, here in Athens we are all totally dependent on a man, father, brother, husband, son, according to the circumstances. A woman who wants power can only have it by having power over this man – except in religion, obviously, where we have our own independent power. Daphne doesn't have any power over her brother. And Daphne's mother was used to having power over her husband – and her father before that, I shouldn't wonder, she knows how to manipulate men. Now she's living in her stepson's house, knowing he hates her, and she doesn't want to get married again because she's become used to living in luxury – the family is extremely rich – and at her age, and with her history, she can't hope to marry someone rich enough for that. Of course, when her son grows up all that will change, and she will be fine again. And even before that, pretty soon Daphne will get married, and she'll twist her husband round her little finger, and then she will have all the power she wants, and her mother with her. But at the moment they are biding their time, waiting for the right victim."

The two women walked in silence; eventually Mego said, "You know, you've been talking a lot about love, and about people marrying for love?"

"Yes?"

"Well, I was under the impression that all marriages were arranged."

Chloe laughed. "Ah, well, that's another complicated story. I don't know about Sparta, but here, there are two parallel fictions about marriage. The first is that marriage is about erotic love. The ritual, the images, they all express the idea that marriage is about people falling in love and having an erotic sexual union. But then there is the second fiction, which many people see as the reality, because this is what fits their idea of what reality is: in this all marriages are arranged, for practical reasons, and all this erotic stuff is just official ideology that hides reality."

"And that's not true?"

"It is true, but it's not the whole story. They may be arranged, but many are arranged because the young people have fallen in love. Not just the young man, the girl too. A father will try to please his daughter if he can. But of course, again, a girl will fall in love with someone among the young men she meets, and that's usually family, or family friends, or her friends' family, and mostly that's a suitable partner anyway. They do see unknown youths at the various festivals, but I think you don't fall in love with people who don't meet certain unthinking expectations, and most people's expectations are the ones set by society. Equally, if you are ugly, you don't generally fall in love with the most beautiful youth in town, unless you've got other things to compensate. Of course sometimes exactly the opposite happens, but I think that's very rare, and that's when we have the stories of destructive catastrophic love sent by the gods to punish people who have offended them, like Phaedra's love for her stepson, which destroyed them both..." She stopped and then added, somewhat self-consciously, "That's my theory, anyway."

"It's a fascinating theory. I hadn't thought about it like that before." Mego said. They walked on in silence. When they rejoined the girls Anthea was taunting Daphne. "I'm surprised that you are so fond of Melissa all of a sudden, Daphne. She hasn't got a brother, or didn't you know that? You are wasting your time making up to her."

Daphne was stung. "I am not making up to her! I don't need to ingratiate myself with anyone's little sister, not like you creeps. I don't need to run after any man. Men run after me."

Anthea ignored Daphne's comment. "Of course," she went on, in a tone that suggested she was giving the matter serious thought, "though Melissa hasn't got a brother, she does have a cousin who is not at all bad looking. And he's the priestess' son. Maybe," she turned to Electra and Helena, pretending sudden illumination, "she is killing two birds with one stone, ingratiating herself with the priestess as well."

Daphne was furious. "I don't need to ingratiate myself with anyone," she said shrilly. "People make up to me; I don't need to make up to them. But you wouldn't understand that. All your life you've been sucking up to someone or other. I don't need to do that."

"Are you saying that the priestess Theano is making up to you? Is that what you are saying?"

"I didn't say that. And for your information, Melissa is not the priestess' niece, she's her husband's niece, so why should she care?"

"Oh yea, and how do you know that, then?"

"Because Melissa told me her father's brother is married to the priestess. It's Melissa who is hanging around me, not the other way round. She's obviously got a crush on me. But you wouldn't know. Not even a little girl could have a crush on any of you." She turned her back on the other girls contemptuously

25

and walked away.

'I am going to have to pay for this, eventually', Electra thought. But she said nothing. She knew that Anthea had meant well.

Chapter Three

Mego decided to wander around on her own for a little while. She had listened to Chloe's talk about the sanctuary and its buildings earlier – well, to some of it – but she hadn't really looked; she should make an effort to take in her surroundings, get to know the sanctuary, not let everything wash over her as though she had never left Sparta – though it's true that the various dramas involving the girls had grabbed her attention for a time. Buildings didn't excite her all that much at the best of times, but maybe she would surprise her husband by telling him about the sanctuary. She knew that things had not been easy for him either, and that she shouldn't have been shutting him out, but she hadn't been able to do anything else. Yes, she would write to him and tell him about the sanctuary, something that she knew would interest him.

The temple dominates the sanctuary, she would tell him. There are, in fact, two temples, but the old temple is now a Treasury, where they store some of the precious offerings dedicated by the worshipers, golden and silver cups and other vessels, bronze incense burners, elegant furniture decorated with gold and ivory, ivory thrones, ivory combs and chests, necklaces and other jewellery, gold, silver and bronze mirrors. It's a rich sanctuary, she would tell him. There are two statues of the goddess in the temple, the marble statue, and an ancient wooden one, which is especially holy, because it was brought here by Iphigeneia, the daughter of Agamemnon, who founded this

27

sanctuary when she escaped from the barbarians, after her father had sacrificed her to Artemis – or so he thought.

The altar is in front of the temple to the east, as always. To the north there is a large three-winged porticoed building, with dining suites for ritual meals; apparently during the festival the most important officials of the Athenian state dine there. There are statues dedicated by worshippers everywhere. There is also an ancient spring, sacred to the goddess, where people throw offerings, mostly women, of course, since Artemis Brauronia has a special responsibility for women and child-rearing.

Mego thought that was enough for one day. She returned to the building where they all lived, the bears and the women guests, and the priestly personnel – except for the priestess herself, who lived in the house of the priestess. It was called 'the amphipoleion', and it was a large two-storeyed house, built around an inner courtyard; a colonnade ran around it on the ground floor, forming a deep shaded portico dotted with benches and potted plants.

They had an early dinner, for they would all be getting up very early the next morning, Chloe explained to Mego, because the bears were going to perform a ritual called the Sacred Hunt. They ate in the courtyard; they had fish that had just come out of the sea this morning, grilled on charcoals, with olive oil. The succulent white flesh made Mego feel her tongue burst with pleasure. Sparta is a long way from the sea, and this was a rare experience for her.

The girls were bickering throughout dinner, the four older ones with some venom, aroused by Daphne's scornful remarks about Electra's alleged unattractiveness to men, to which Anthea and Helena responded in kind, Helena telling Daphne that she was the one who was a loser. "You need to get a life," she added.

"And she needs to get a husband, but she can't." Daphne

said, mockingly, of Electra. "Only if they force one of her relatives."

"That's how much you know," Anthea countered, trying to look knowing. "But then, what do you expect, how would you know what's going on? No one talks to you who doesn't have to. Except little girls with crushes."

Helena, who realized what Anthea was doing, strengthened the credibility of the fiction, by saying what she would have said if it had been true. "Don't tell her, you don't want her to know, she'd put the evil eye on them."

Chloe did not intervene, Mego noticed. After they had finished dinner and the girls had gone inside, Chloe sat on a bench by the entrance. "It's difficult to remember that things like that meant life and death at that age," she said to Mego. "Oh, well…" She sighed.

Mego joined her on the bench. "How old are you now?" she asked. She thought that Chloe's remark had given her an opening to ask.

"Thirty-four."

"And you never married…" she let the sentence hang between a question and a statement. Chloe didn't have to say anything if she didn't want to.

"I was engaged to be married once, but he left me."

"Were you in love with him?"

"Oh yes, I was. Indeed I was."

"Did he love you? At the beginning?"

Chloe sighed. "I thought he did, but I was obviously wrong. I used to tell myself that it was family pressure that made him leave me virtually at the altar, but even if that were true, it wouldn't make it much better, would it? He married someone else, of course."

"Couldn't you have married someone else?"

29

"Ah, well, maybe, and maybe not. It's a long story... Anyway ...I do like this job. And I can support myself; I don't have to depend on my brother. So..."

"I see..." Just as Mego realized that she should back off, she saw a woman with the short hair of a slave rushing in their direction.

"Theano wants to see you," she told Chloe. "She says she's worried about the Sacred Hunt. I told her that the clothes are ready to be taken to the woods at dawn and that everything else is under control, and that there's nothing else to be done at this stage, but she still wants to see you. Now, apparently."

"It's not really about the Hunt she's fretting," Chloe said to Mego. "It's about the bears and their discipline. She can't see that they were far too excited so close to the festival, and with the Sacred Hunt tomorrow, to have proper lessons today, even for music and poetry, let alone weaving at the loom, which is what she wanted. A bit of physical exercise is all you can get them to do at this stage. But no, Theano thinks I'm too soft on them."

Chloe left; the slave woman stayed behind. "Should I ask what this Sacred Hunt is or is it a secret rite strangers aren't supposed to know about?" Mego asked her.

"Oh no, it's not a secret, anything but. But I think you'd better wait and see it for yourself tomorrow. I wouldn't want to spoil the surprise. Actually, it doesn't sound much when you just describe it."

"Right then. I'll be looking forward to seeing it. Thanks. Ahhm ...I'm sorry, I don't know your name."

"Bakchis."

"I am Mego, the priestess of Artemis Orthia at Sparta."

"Yes, I know." She made to go, but then she turned back, and said, "It just occurred to me, there are some things I could tell you about tomorrow, so that you'll know what to expect, in case no one else has thought of explaining. The Hunt takes place in a wooded hill, not far from here, and it's a big public occasion. Everyone staying at the sanctuary will be there, and the bears' families and the helpers' families and anyone else who wants to watch. Usually lots of people turn up."

"Really? Where do they come from? We are a long way from the city of Athens here."

"Many are locals, but there are others too, like the girls' families as I said. They stay with friends or family who have houses in the area, or a bit further away; many places along the coast are just a short boat ride away, or a short ride. So they come up before the Sacred Hunt and they stay until after the festival."

"It sounds quite interesting."

"Oh yes, it is, you'll see. Well, good night, then." She turned to go, adding "You'd better get a good night's sleep. You'll need it for tomorrow."

As it turned out Mego didn't get a good night's sleep, at least not an uninterrupted one; she was woken up in the middle of the night – or so it seemed, it was certainly totally dark – by noises and whispers coming from underneath her window. Her room was over the porch, but she couldn't imagine who would be up and about and out in the porch at this hour. Eventually, among the jumbled images of pre-sleep into which she had begun to slide, she thought she heard a male voice. 'Dream or real', she told herself, as she was sinking back into sleep, 'Chloe will deal with it.' But in this she was wrong. Chloe had been summoned by Theano to discuss the details of the Hunt yet again. And as Theano lived in the house of the priestess, Chloe didn't hear what Mego had heard, and she didn't know that there was anything that needed dealing with. Which, as it turned out, was very unfortunate.

31

Chapter Four

They set out just after dawn the next day – Chloe, Theano, Mego, the bears and the older girls, Bakchis and a few other slaves. Most of the sanctuary slaves had gone before, with the donkeys loaded with the sacred clothes and various necessary provisions.

Theano was wearing a purple robe and a black and gold mantle, and she had an ornate diadem on her head and a gold pendant around her neck. She had been bustling and fussing from the moment she had come out of her house. "It is I who am the priestess and it is my responsibility if anything goes wrong," she was telling Chloe. "It is my name, and my husband's name and my son's name that are on the line here. It is I who will be judged. No one is going to be blaming you, they don't know you, I am the priestess. So if I want to go over it again and again, no one is going to stop me. If you want to get a job done properly you've got to do it yourself."

"Why don't you, then?" Mego heard Bakchis mutter.

They didn't have as far to walk as Mego had feared. The wood was up the slope of a hill not very far from the sanctuary. Some parts of the wood were dense, but in other places you could see some considerable distance ahead between the trees, and the dappled sunlight opened up into pools. As the sun got stronger they were hit by swirls of smells oozing out off the trees, the bushes and the undergrowth. After a bit the slope got a little steep, and Mego paused to catch her breath. No one noticed that she had fallen behind, and she thought she wouldn't get lost if she walked a bit more slowly, as long as she could see the tail-end of the group of bears who were ahead of her.

But not all the bears were ahead of her, she suddenly realized, when she heard angry voices, little girls' angry voices, coming from behind a dense clump of pine trees on her right.

"You are going to do it, and that's that," one of them said.

"No I am not. I told you I am not going to do it."

"Oh yes, you are. You'll do exactly as I say."

"I told you. I am not going to do it, not this time. This matters too much to me. Whatever happens today, I am going to try to win the race at the festival."

"I may win anyway."

"I know, and that's fine – well, not fine, but okay. There's nothing I can do about that. It may be you, or it may be me. Or it could be someone else."

"No, you know very well that there's no one else apart from you that's serious competition for me."

"Whatever. I know you are a good archer and a good runner. But I am going to try to win. If I lose I lose. But I am going to try."

"You'll do as I say or I am going to tell."

"Go ahead …tell. I'm sick of it. I've had enough. I shouldn't have let you do it to me in the first place. Bullies never stop. Eunice was right."

"Oh, Eunice was right, was she? So you told her the truth did you?" When the other girl didn't reply she went on. "No, I thought not. Never you mind, I'll tell her. I'll tell everyone that your father hasn't got any money left, and you are poor."

"We are not poor!"

"Oh yes, you are poor, and I'll tell everyone. Then we'll see who wants to be your friend."

"And I'll tell you've been sneaking out at night and stealing figs from the orchard next door. I saw you again last night, sneaking out. You were out half the night. I don't suppose the poor man has got any figs left on his trees."

The other girl laughed triumphantly. "You can't do that. You can't tell on me. That would be dobbing. No one will talk to you ever again if you dob."

'Oh, Lord, no…!' thought Mego. 'This sounds like serious bullying, in fact, blackmail. What should I do about it? I'm sure Chloe doesn't need this dropped on her lap just now, I certainly wouldn't in her position; so I suppose there is nothing I can do until this is over.' She didn't think it would be necessary to try to identify the two girls; she thought Chloe would know who they were when Mego repeated their conversation, in fact even Mego herself could make a guess after she heard what they were saying about the race.

Ahead of her the main group was slowing down and Mego caught up with them as they came to a large man-made clearing. This clearing was encircled by a belt of thinned out wood with no undergrowth. There were a lot of people there already, in this section around the clearing, standing, or sitting on camp-stools, or lying on the ground, or on brightly coloured cushions and mattresses. There were trays of fruit and cakes and jugs of wine on the tables and on the ground. At the edge of the clearing there were two long tables and several large chests; the sanctuary slaves were taking bows and quivers full of arrows out of the chests and putting them on the tables. Each bear picked up a bow and a quiver. They played about a bit, until Chloe gave them a command, then they formed four lines, each ten girls deep. Each line was facing one of the trees at the opposite end of the clearing, on each of which there was an arrangement of metal and wooden parts that held a bronze plaque with a hole in the middle at a certain distance from the tree trunk.

People started to get up and press forward to stand around the perimeter of the clearing, as a flute player appeared and walked around playing a hymn. He was wearing a long white robe with large patterns in red and yellow woven into the fabric. He stopped next to Theano, and as he stopped the first bear on each line drew her bow. Theano stepped out, raised her hands, said a short prayer to Artemis, and then announced the beginning of the shooting competition. The bears had to shoot the arrow through the hole and into the trunk of the tree.

The first four girls did not manage to drive the arrow into the tree, and neither did most of the others that followed. At the end of the first round only a small group had been successful. This group, which included both Kallisto and Melissa, lined up for the second round, standing much further back, among the trees. Melissa drew first, but her shot was clumsy and she was eliminated, as were eventually all the others, one by one, until only Kallisto was left. All eyes were on her. There was a hush. Everyone knew that this was now serious. If Kallisto didn't manage to shoot the arrow through the hole and embed it into the tree they would have to start again nearer the target, and that was not going to be a good omen for the city or for the girls themselves.

Kallisto was shaking. She bit her lips hard, so that the pain would steady her hands. She drew the bow, and fired; the arrow sailed through the hole in the plaque and buried itself in the tree. The crowd cheered. Kallisto burst into tears. Electra made to rush to her, but Anthea grabbed her arm and held her back. Chloe went up to Kallisto, took her by the hand and led her to the middle of the clearing, where Theano now stood, next to an open chest and a low table.

The flute player started playing, and a group of bears sang a choral song. Theano took away Kallisto's bow and arrow and gave them to a slave, then she picked up the little girl and placed her on the table. She undressed her, then carefully took out of the chest a short robe, white with gold embroidery, displayed it to the bears and the spectators, and then put it on the girl. The embroidered images showed Artemis and her companions hunting deer. There were also inscriptions in gold that said who had dedicated the robe to Artemis. Theano then put a wreath of flowers on Kallisto's head. Kallisto jumped off the table and went to stand next to Chloe, who was handing out white dresses with gold embroidered borders, and gold inscriptions, to a group of bears which included Melissa and all the other girls who had made it to the second round. They took off their saffron robes and changed into what were clearly the sacred clothes that had been brought from the sanctuary. They came to stand next to Theano and Chloe, while the girls who were still wearing the saffron yellow clothes formed a circle. They danced an elaborate dance in and out of the clearing, in and out of the trees. They sang a hymn to Artemis. When they finished, they stood at one end of the clearing while Kallisto's group moved to the centre. Theano seemed to have disappeared.

Chloe stood in front of Kallisto and gave her a new gilded bow and a quiver which she had taken out of a purple bag. Then she lifted her hand and uttered a prayer for the success of the hunt. Kallisto drew her bow and shot an arrow in the air. The others followed. The crowd parted and Kallisto led her band up the slope, running through the trees.

"The deer are higher up the slope," Electra explained to Mego. "I do hope Kallisto manages to kill at least a fawn. It's very bad luck when they don't, you know."

"Yes, I would imagine it would be..." Mego replied. As she thought, the basic mentality of these rituals was the same everywhere in Greece. "What happens now? Do we wait until they get back?"

"Look." Anthea pointed towards a clump of trees on the other side of the clearing. Something seemed to be moving there, very slowly. At the centre of the clearing the larger group of bears that had not gone hunting were sitting on the ground in little circles, throwing knucklebones. The flute player began to play again. The bears looked up as though startled. They were looking in the direction of the trees where Mego had seen that slow movement. Something large and four-legged emerged slowly from the trees. After a few steps it stopped, it growled and then it stepped into a pool of sunlight and stood on its hind legs. It was a woman wearing a bear mask.

"It's Theano, as I'm sure you guessed," Anthea told Mego. The woman in the bear mask came up to the little girls, slowly and tentatively. She was wearing bear paws over her hands. The girls didn't move. The make-believe animal stretched out an arm and made as though to touch one of them. The girls jumped up and started running around her, pushing her and hitting her lightly. She tried to get away but they wouldn't let her. Their movements became more frenzied and their shouts louder. Suddenly she growled and lurched at one of the girls and scratched her arm so that blood ran out. The girl screamed. The others pulled back and the woman in the bear mask ran away into the woods, up the slope.

"This is the story of the bear who got killed because she hurt a little girl when she got excited while they were playing together, which is why we have to be bears to make amends to the goddess. But, of course, what you just saw isn't the story as it happened. In our story the men don't come and the bear doesn't get killed," Electra explained.

"Do you remember," Daphne said to Helena, "when it was

37

you who got scratched when we did it, and you wouldn't stop crying afterwards? I bet the priestess chose you on purpose to scratch, because you were always such a cry baby."

"You weren't such a hotshot yourself, Daphne, I seem to remember," Anthea cut in. "If you had been any good you'd have been out hunting with the goddess, as I was."

"Were you one of the hunters too?" Mego asked Electra.

"Yes, I was." Electra blushed.

"Actually, it was Electra who played the goddess in our year. She is an excellent shot." Anthea put her arm around her friend. Then she looked towards the clearing and whooped "Aah… Food at last. I'm starving."

Bakchis and another slave came up bringing trays of honey cakes, jugs of water and cups. They set them on the ground. Daphne grabbed a tray and a jug and ran away among the trees.

"She can't stand not getting as much as she wants of whatever's going." Electra said.

"No, it's our company she doesn't fancy, I think," Anthea didn't seem deeply wounded by this.

"But she was nice last night," Helena felt obliged to remind them, "She did go and fetch the wine for us."

Electra wasn't prepared to concede any points. "She probably drank most of it, that's why," she said.

"Ah, that I'm not so sure about," Anthea said, teasingly. "It wasn't Daphne who slept like the dead and had to be dragged out of bed this morning by the leg."

"That wasn't just me. You weren't any better yourself. And Helena."

"Yes, I know." She stopped and seemed to be considering something. "You know, that's what's bizarre. The three of us, but not Daphne."

"I must say I haven't felt like that, like I had rocks on my head, since last year, when I had the fever," Helena admitted.

"So, what are you saying, Anthea?" Electra prompted her friend to spell things out.

"You know what I'm saying. She must have drugged our wine, that's why she went to fetch it. She was probably meeting some man and she didn't want us to know she'd gone."

Mego remembered the male voice she'd thought she'd heard in the night. She hadn't drunk the wine Daphne had brought her. She didn't like wine last thing at night, but of course she hadn't told Daphne that. She had wondered why it had been Daphne who was taking the wine round, and not one of the slaves, and she'd asked, but Daphne had said that Theano didn't want the slaves to go to the storerooms alone after nightfall, when they could steal things and cart them away with no one seeing them. Obviously, that was another thing Chloe had to be told about – if she didn't know already, that is, and another thing that would have to wait. At the moment Chloe seemed busy talking to some of the spectators on the other side of the clearing. The bears who had taken part in the performance were messing around, jumping about, cartwheeling and lying on the ground. When the slaves brought them trays and jugs and cups they calmed down and fell on the food. The spectators were milling around, eating and drinking and talking.

Suddenly Electra jumped up and stood staring rigidly at a group on the other side of the clearing. Anthea noticed. "What's the matter?" she asked.

"Do you see my father over there?" Electra asked. "Do you see who he is with?"

"Your grandmother."

"No, no, not my grandmother, the young man behind him?"

"Yes, I see him, not bad looking, very fit. What's wrong? Who is he?"

"He's my cousin, Charias, my father's brother's son. The man who can claim me in marriage even if I am married to someone else. What is he doing with my father?"

"Watching the Hunt, I should think."

"No, you don't understand. There is no reason why he should be with my father, unless he wants something. They aren't close, and he lives on the other side of the city, in the Piraeus; so what is he doing here, and why should my father bring him to the Hunt?"

"You think it's something to do with you? His claim on you?"

"What else can it be? They have nothing else to do with each other. So much for my father's promises. He promised me that he would look after me, that he wouldn't force me to marry my cousin or anyone I didn't want to. So what is he doing bringing him to the Hunt?"

"It may be nothing to do with you. You mustn't jump to the blackest conclusions all the time. It could be something to do with things you know nothing about, a political alliance or something like that."

"You think? With my luck…"

"Are you going to go over and talk to them?"

"Absolutely not."

"You may be able to find out something if you go over."

"I don't want to give Charias the impression I am encouraging him, in fact I don't want to see him at all."

"Why, do you hate him? Is he horrible?"

"No, no, of course I don't hate him, and he's not horrible at all. In fact, I quite liked him when we were children, and we used to see more of each other; it made me feel important that so many girls were attracted to him and he was my cousin."

"Yes, he's quite a hunk."

"But I just don't want to marry him." Electra now started sounding hysterical. "The idea makes me sick."

"I still think you should go over and try to find out what's going on."

"To tell you the truth, if the news is bad, I'd rather not know until I have to."

"But that's silly; it's going to be eating you up in the meantime."

"At least I won't be sure."

"But it may not be what you think it is. And even if it is, you could do something about it if you knew for sure."

"No, I couldn't. There's nothing I could do. If my father has decided that I've got to marry Charias, that's that. And it's not as though Kallias has been beating a path to my door to take me away from it all, is it? No, there's nothing I can do. Other than kill myself."

"Oh, for the goddess' sake, Electra, don't be ridiculous."

"Why am I being ridiculous? What is there to live for?"

Mego knew that what seemed absurd to a rational human being was perfectly reasonable to a lovesick adolescent, whose vision was limited to her obsessive concerns. So she was not inclined to assume that Electra's talk about suicide could be lightly dismissed as melodrama – not necessarily. She wondered how much of all this Chloe knew. And then she wondered how much she herself may not know about the people around her in her own sanctuary at Sparta.

"Come and meet my family and have some refreshments with us." Mego realized that Theano had come up behind her.

'So the priestess did feel she had to make some effort', Mego thought, as she smiled politely. "Thank you, I would like that very much."

"My son is not here, of course," Theano was talking as she

41

was leading the way across the clearing, "he is doing his ephebic service. Here things are different from Sparta, we don't have the long training that you have for our boys, they just go off for two years' military service, as it were, at eighteen; they spend one year in the barracks in the Piraeus and one year in a frontier post. Alexias is at Rhamnous, a sort of garrison town on the coast north of here." She led Mego to a small group centred around a man sitting up on a litter, with his head on cushions that rested against the thick trunk of a tree. The others were sitting on camp-stools. "This is my husband, Nikias," Theano said, gesturing to a tall faired-haired man in his forties with a neat beard and a well-muscled body. "And this is my daughter Kleopatra and her husband Phanes." Kleopatra was a young woman in her twenties who looked like Theano, only not quite so attractive, more thin-faced; her husband was a young man with mousy hair, a broadish face and brown eyes, who looked in every way unexceptional. "And this is my sister-in-law, Hermione. Her daughter, Melissa, is one of our graduating bears." Hermione had faded blonde hair, and one could say, Mego thought, she was a faded blonde person, with a faded blonde voice that spoke appropriate faded blonde things. 'Don't be bitchy', Mego chided herself. 'She can't help it. And the poor woman's life can't be easy.' The man on the litter was Hermione's husband, Nikias' brother, Leandros. He had been paralysed for eight years, ever since he had been attacked and almost killed by a wild boar while hunting, as he informed Mego, before launching into a series of hunting stories, each seamlessly following the other, and involving detailed descriptions of the various dogs Leandros had possessed at the time. A young slave ladled wine from a large mixing bowl into a jug and filled their cups.

The mix was weak, with a lot of water, but at that time of the day, together with Leandros' voice, it had a strongly soporific

42

effect, at least on Mego.

Afterwards she wasn't sure if she had fallen asleep. Suddenly a slave came running up to Nikias and whispered something in his ear; Nikias jumped up and followed the slave down the slope. Theano looked thunderous, but she couldn't very well run after him. Or indeed show her annoyance. "I should introduce you to some more people," she said to Mego. "The little girl impersonating the goddess, Kallisto, that's her family over there." She gestured towards a group that were strolling by with two children in tow. "That's her father, the elderly woman is her grandmother, the man with the children is her elder brother with his wife and sons, and the beautiful dark-haired youth is her brother Kallias. They are one of our best families. Shall I call them over? Oh …oh…" she said in a different tone, looking behind Mego. "Here comes someone who wants to hook you and show off what big fishes swim in her little pond. Daphne's mother, Olympias, is coming our way."

Mego saw a short, fair-haired woman approaching, her face set into a huge smile. She was heavily made up and gaudily dressed, and she had come to invite Mego to join her and her friends. Mego accepted the invitation and went over. This is what she was here for, basically, wasn't she? – to watch other people's lives.

"We all heard of your visit. It's such a great honour to meet you, priestess Mego. Will you be staying long?" Olympias said as they were walking away from Theano's family.

"I will be staying for the festival, of course. Then I'll probably be going back to the city straight away."

"And will you be stopping over in the city?"

"Oh yes, I'll be staying for a few days."

"In that case you must definitely come and visit us when we get back. We live in Melite, right in the centre. You must come

43

and have dinner with the family. We will give you the most sumptuous meal you've ever had. We can fix a day now, if you like."

"That's very kind of you," Mego answered, "but I'm afraid I will have to check what official engagements have been arranged for me before I let you know."

"Yes, of course, I understand. Just send a message to me at the house of Stephanos, son of Satyros from Melite …it's my stepson's house, strictly speaking. As soon as you know."

"Thank you, I will remember that."

"You've met my daughter Daphne, I expect. She's one of the helpers in the sanctuary, which is a great honour. Isn't she the most beautiful girl you've ever seen?"

"She's extremely beautiful, yes. You must be very proud of her."

"Oh, I am, I am indeed. And she will have a huge dowry as well."

"That's nice," Mego said. She had met people like that before, but it was always embarrassing. She looked around trying to think of something else to say, and saw an elderly lady reclining on purple cushions set on a gold and red mattress apparently summoning them to her side, patting a cushion next to her.

"That lady over there seems to be calling us over," she told Olympias.

"Oh, shit! That's my sister-in-law. She is so totally boring, you don't want to be stuck with her."

"It doesn't look as though I have a choice," Mego replied. "Not a polite one, anyway." She went over and smiled at the elderly lady, who smiled back and said "Good morning priestess Mego. I am Praxilla, Daphne's aunt; her late father's sister. Come and sit next to me so we can have a nice chat."

44

As Mego joined Praxilla, Olympias ordered a middle aged balding man whom she addressed as Andreas to bring her a stool; when he did she sat down next to Mego. "I am sorry you won't be able to meet my son, Philippos," she said to Mego. "He wasn't feeling very well when we all woke up at dawn and I let him stay home and lie in."

"If he was prepared to miss the Hunt he must be really ill," said Praxilla. "He is smitten with one of the bears," she explained to Mego.

"So you keep saying," Olympias snapped.

"So is blindingly obvious, even if I don't yet know who the girl is; I'm surprised you can deny it, they do say none so blind... He's been like a lovesick puppy, certainly in the last few days, since we came to stay at your father's house; I would have thought someone like you with your extensive knowledge of such things..."

"And what do you mean by that?"

"Your knowledge of human character, my dear. What did you think I meant? But my point is that if Philippos was unwell enough not to want to come to the Hunt, there's something seriously wrong, and you shouldn't have left him alone."

"He's not alone, as you very well know. My father is there as well. My father, Philon, has seen the Hunt so many times, living nearby," she explained to Mego, "that he can't be bothered to come any more. Anyway, Philippos is twelve years old, he's not a baby."

"But he's clearly ill, and it could be really serious. I do hope he hasn't caught the fever from me. I've just recovered from a really bad fever, you know," she explained to Mego. "There, you see, I still have some boils around the ears, but at least they aren't full of puss any more. And the bilious diarrhoea has stopped."

"You said you are Daphne's father's sister." Mego tried to change the subject; everyone else around them was trying to eat, and she herself had intended to try some white grapes. "Younger sister, I presume."

"Oh, no, no …I am his older sister, much older sister. Mind you, I'm the one who's still here and he's been gone three years now, but then I take an interest in my body. My brother would never listen. I told him it was serious, when he first got ill, I told him I'd seen exactly the same thing, when our uncle's wife was sick, just before she died, the same vomit, full of bile, phlegm, and food; and his urine was muddy. And then I saw his stools, and they were black, and that's always a sign of death."

"Ah, there is our friend Kriton," Olympias exclaimed as loudly as she thought one could without making a spectacle of oneself. "Let's call him over. I am surprised to see him on his own on a day like this."

"If he's on his own," Praxilla said, "it means that his wife couldn't come because their son got worse; their youngest son has the dropsy," she explained to Mego. "I had a friend whose daughter had the dropsy, and her body filled up with water and…"

The booming voice of a raven-haired woman cut in, "and speaking of absent friends, where is our dear Stephanos, why hasn't he joined us yet?"

Olympias didn't quite suppress her fury. "You know very well, Alexandra," she said to the woman, "that he's got his duties to perform as one of the overseers of the sacred rites. I am sure he'll be joining us as soon as he's free." She got up and busied herself with some trays of fruit, which she rearranged on one of the tables.

"Stephanos is my nephew, Daphne's brother, half-brother I should say," Praxilla explained to Mego, a glint in her brown,

46

cow-like eyes. "That was a dig at Olympias. Alexandra is married to my cousin's son, but her brother, Andreas, is besotted with Olympias, you saw him earlier, jumping to obey her commands; that's why she hangs around, Alexandra, to keep an eye on things. She's obsessed with protecting her little brother from predatory women – not that I can really blame her where Olympias concerned. Anyway, she knows very well that Stephanos won't be joining us, not even for the sake of appearances. Mind you, what appearances? Everyone knows how things stand; he hates Olympias because he thinks it's her fault his mother died, that his father leaving her was what killed his mother. And I can't say I blame him. My brother was always a fool, even since he was little; so full of himself that anyone could twist him round their little fingers if they played on his vanity. And Daphne's mother is a master, or should I say mistress?" Her laughter was interrupted by Olympias herself, who had crept up to them.

"Poor Stephanos is extremely busy," she said to Mego. "He has a very important job to do. Otherwise of course he would be here, he adores his little sister. Not that Daphne is here, obviously. The helpers never join their families. Not that they are not allowed to, but they always want to make it clear that they are members of the sanctuary staff, and have things to do. I was the same at their age."

"Don't believe a word of it," Praxilla said to Mego after Olympias had left again, to join Andreas. She had obviously only come over to inform Mego of Stephanos' adoration for Daphne. "She was never a helper in the sanctuary, as she wanted to make you think. She hadn't even been a bear. She's just a local girl; her family were not good enough for her to be chosen. I told you, my brother was a fool."

"You all keep talking about good families and not good

enough families. I thought Athens was a democracy, and that it was governed by the will of the people."

"But of course it is. What has that got to do with anything?" Praxilla sounded surprised.

Before Mego could reply, she saw Chloe waving at her from the other side of the clearing, and so she took her leave of Praxilla and went over to join the subpriestess.

"All my duties are over for the time being," Chloe said, "and I thought you might like to go for a little walk, to stretch your legs."

"I wouldn't mind, now you mention it, just for a few minutes. I am feeling a bit stiff, I now realize."

They walked up a gentle part of the slope. "None of your family are here, I take it," Mego said.

"No…" Chloe hesitated, and then went on. "Not that I have much family left."

"I thought you mentioned a brother."

"Yes, I have a half-brother, from my mother's first marriage, Melanthios. He's my legal guardian; as I told you; Athenian women have to have a legal guardian to represent us in court, and so on, just like minors. And my mother is still alive; but my father was convicted of treason, he tried to flee the country and he died trying. And our other relatives do not exactly force themselves on me to claim our kinship."

"Oh, I am so sorry…" Mego touched Chloe's upper arm in a gesture of sympathy.

Chloe sat down on one of the boulders that dotted the slope. "I don't know if my father was a traitor or not. Maybe it was as clear cut as they said in court, maybe not. But right or wrong, I am not allowed to forget it for very long."

"Is that why your fiancé left you?"

"That and the fact that I no longer came from a well-off

family, since everything my father had owned was sold off, and I didn't have a good dowry any more."

It was Mego's turn to feel she didn't know what to say, and to say the obvious. "Oh, my dear, I am so sorry. You've had really tough experiences at an early age, haven't you?"

"I am fine now. I told you, I like this job. And I can support myself."

"Do you get on well with your brother?"

"Well enough. But our relations are amicable, rather than close. When I am not in the sanctuary – which isn't very often, unlike Theano, I spend most of my time here – I stay in his house." Suddenly, Chloe jumped up. "Let's get back. The girls are returning from the Hunt."

Little by little what had seemed to be a faint humming noise in the background became the sound of girls' voices singing. A procession could be glimpsed among the trees coming down the slope. The bears were returning from the Hunt, carrying the stag they had killed – Kallisto had killed – and singing a hymn to the goddess. Kallisto was at the head of the procession and the woman in the bear mask walked next to her.

They came and stood at the centre of the clearing. Theano removed the bear mask and paws. Then, first Kallisto and then the other girls washed in water brought to them in bowls by the slaves and then changed back into their ordinary saffron coloured dresses and formed a circle around the animal. Theano said a prayer over the stag. She asked Artemis and the other gods to grant prosperity to the city as they had granted success in the Hunt, and to protect the bears in their future life and make them good Athenian wives and mothers for the better glory of the city. The bears and the teenagers uttered a shrill ritual cry. Then it was all over.

Chapter Five

The spectators were beginning to leave. Two sanctuary slaves tied up the stag on a low wheeled platform for carrying it to the sanctuary, while the others were packing up the sacred clothes and the rest of the things that had to be taken back. The bears were restless, running about, screaming and bickering. Chloe wished that Theano would hurry, so they could get moving. She looked around to make sure that all the girls were ready to go and saw that not everyone was where they ought to be.

"Daphne is not here. Do you know where she's gone?" she asked the three older girls.

"No, we haven't seen her since she grabbed a tray and a jug and disappeared, when they brought the honey cakes. At least I haven't. Have you?" Anthea asked the other two, who confirmed that they hadn't seen her since she'd disappeared with the honey cakes.

"She may be with her mother and she's forgotten that she was supposed to be back," Theano suggested.

"Yea, right..." Anthea said under her breath. The girls giggled. Chloe explained that the eventuality was extremely remote, but Theano insisted on sending someone to check. The messenger returned with the information that Daphne's mother and her friends had left without Daphne, and that her aunt, whom they had caught as she was leaving with some friends, said that they hadn't seen her at all that day; she hadn't gone near her mother or anyone else in her mother's party.

"Trust that silly girl to make trouble at the Sacred Hunt," Theano muttered.

"She's not that silly," Chloe told her. "And I know her. She wouldn't have drawn attention to herself if she could help it. She must have got lost in the woods."

"How could she be so stupid?" Theano was annoyed; she obviously thought that Chloe was right. "And why was she wandering in the woods on her own in the first place?"

"As to that I could venture a guess, but this is not the moment to discuss it. We must try to find her first."

"She means she was meeting a man. And I bet she was." Electra' hadn't tried to make her voice inaudible.

Theano heard her and was incensed. She turned on Chloe. "This is all your fault. I told you, you are too lax with them. All of them. None of this would have happened if there had been proper discipline. But no, you always know best."

Chloe tried to keep herself under control. "Maybe you are right, maybe I am too lax. But then I am not normally used to dealing with girls of Daphne's sort. It was your choice, not mine, to have her back here as one of the helpers. I warned you at the time. But of course you wouldn't listen."

"And what exactly do you mean by 'girls of her sort', may I ask? Her family is very respectable and extremely wealthy."

"Never mind now. This is not the time."

"No, you are not getting out of it as easily as that. Since you chose to make the sanctuary's affairs public knowledge you'd better make yourself clear, you can't just bandy about vague accusations to avoid blame."

Chloe's sense of discretion – such as it was – evaporated under the onslaught. "You want me to be specific in public; I'll be specific in public. Daphne is a manipulative little tart, just like her mother."

"How dare you?" Theano shrieked. "How dare you say such a thing? And in front of everyone. Well, that's torn it. I've had more than enough of you. This time I will have you dismissed, see if I don't."

Chloe was past caring by now. "And I'll tell you something else, Daphne's pregnant. Did you know that? No, of course you didn't. But I did. And so did Bakchis."

Theano blanched and Electra, Anthea and Helena were struck dumb. They clearly hadn't known this. The bears were highly amused. The burst into sniggers and started running around the trees, shrieking and making up silly rhymes about Daphne having a baby. Almost immediately, Theano's stunned dismay turned to fury, displaced, of course, onto Chloe. "If you knew, or thought you knew, because you are probably mistaken, both of you, but if you thought you knew that Daphne was pregnant, why didn't you see fit to tell me about it? I am the priestess, it was my responsibility."

"What was the point of telling you?" Chloe sounded weary. "There was nothing you could have done before the festival. You couldn't dismiss her without causing a scandal and attracting attention to the whole thing. I don't think you would have liked that. There was no point in just worrying you and making you anxious before the festival."

"You should have let me be the judge of that."

Chloe laughed. "Fine. Next time you choose someone against my advice and she turns out to be pregnant I'll let you know immediately."

"How dare you…" Theano exploded.

"I think we should leave all that aside for the moment," Chloe interrupted the priestess, her voice now under control. "We must send out a search party immediately. Two search parties, in fact, there are enough slaves around for that.

Unfortunately, all the spectators have gone, and we can't ask them for help. But first I think the bears ought to be taken back to the sanctuary."

One girl's voice rose shrilly in protest. "I am not going back. I want to help find Daphne. I am going to look for her." Melissa ran away from the group and into the trees and up the slope.

"Oh, shit...!" Chloe was now beyond trying for restraint. "Now we've got to find her as well. Right, I was going to suggest that we start up the slope anyway, and then search the lower part, if we get no results. At least we'll find Melissa quickly. Bloody child. I could kill her with my bare hands."

"I will take the bears back myself." Theano asserted her authority. "With Bakchis and another slave."

"In that case you should make a quick search of the lower wood as you go down," Chloe told her.

Theano didn't reply, but they both knew that she was going to do as Chloe had suggested – she usually did, when her pride wasn't involved, or one of her petty obsessions. But before any of them had started off for their various destinations, they were startled by a piercing scream that went on and on. They ran towards it and they found Melissa, screaming, and they saw what she had seen; down the slope, by a little brook, Daphne was lying on her back, her forehead and the top of her head awash with blood, her body limp and lifeless. Even from that distance, it was clear that she was dead. A young man was kneeling next to her, sobbing, and grabbing her shoulders, and kissing her. Chloe saw that he was Theano's son, Alexias.

Chapter Six

At the sight of her son Theano let out a shriek, while some of the younger bears made to run towards Daphne's body. Kallisto ran in front of them with her friend Eunice and another older girl and stopped them. "Get back! Get back you little fools," she shouted. "You can't go near a corpse, you know that, you'll be polluted, and then you won't be able to carry on with the rites."

In the meantime Mego had grabbed Theano by the wrist and slapped her to stop her screaming. "You've got to get away from here," she told her. "You are a priestess; you can't be exposed to death, especially not now with the festival coming up."

"My son, that's my son with the body," Theano protested, albeit in a deflated voice.

"I'm very sorry to hear it, but there is nothing you can do for him. We've got to leave."

Chloe had been interrogating Melissa, who said that she hadn't gone any nearer Daphne's body than where she was now, that she had started screaming when she'd seen Alexias and the body. She seemed to be in a daze, but there was no reason to believe that she didn't know what she had or hadn't done. "Fine, in that case we must all leave immediately. None of us can come into further contact with a corpse."

"Or its killer," Mego whispered so that she could only be heard by Chloe, who nodded. "Yes, but first we must make sure someone in authority can take over. I'll send one of the slaves to fetch the overseers of the sacred rites who are responsible for the festival. They must try to catch up with them before they've gone too far. You go ahead and get back to the sanctuary with the bears."

After the others had left, Chloe waited at a safe distance from the body and Alexias, who was still cradling it. Eventually, the five overseers of the sacred rites who were present at the Hunt arrived, and Chloe told them what she knew. She felt free to go, but she didn't, she just moved further away from the corpse and Alexias, and stayed to observe the proceedings. The overseers placed Alexias under arrest. The wood was not part of the sanctuary, so the murder was not really sacrilege, but it was one of Artemis' sacred groves, so the overseers of the sacred rites had taken responsibility. As it happened, one of the ten annual overseers, indeed one of the five who were already at the sanctuary, was Stephanos, Daphne's half-brother and legal guardian, so he was handling the situation, and he would eventually lodge the charge of homicide with the magistrate responsible, the archon basileus. Of course, now Stephanos was not going to be able to continue with his duties at the sanctuary, since as a close blood relative he was polluted, and he had to stay away from rites and sanctuaries. He ordered his slaves to carry Daphne's body to the house of her maternal grandfather Philon in the village – obviously, it had to be kept away from the sanctuary, which must be free of pollution at all times.

By now most of the spectators had left, but as soon as they were told of the killing, the overseers had sent their slaves to stop anyone who may still have been around; people who had left late, or who had gone down the slope slowly because they were accompanying elderly relatives. They were to ask them to stay behind, or at least give their names and addresses, so that they could be asked questions as to whether they had seen anything suspicious before or after the killing. It did look like an open and shut case, with the killer caught red-handed, but Stephanos was a careful man; he didn't like to take anything for granted, or to rely on obvious assumptions, he told his two friends, Andron and Charias, who had been with him and had accompanied him when he was summoned. Andron, as it happened, was this year's archon basileus, the magistrate responsible for homicides. He and Charias had been staying at Andron's summer house at Halai Araphenides, which explained Charias' presence at the Hunt that had so worried Electra.

In fact, when eventually all those who were known to have been at the Hunt were interrogated, no one admitted to having seen anything unusual or out of the ordinary.

Daphne's mother and her friends had left long before the body had been discovered, but Praxilla had stayed behind, to talk to an old friend, and her friend's family were now going to take her back to Philon's house. They had left late and they had been walking slowly down the slope; when they reached the bottom of the hill they stopped for a rest. Praxilla's old friend was Kallisto's grandmother, also called Kallisto, the mother of Kallisto's father Kallimachos. They had grown up together, she and Praxilla, and they had been bears together, such a long time ago, Praxilla thought. And today her old friend was showing her years, which she usually didn't, well, not quite so much, anyway. She looked tired and, what was the word? Despondent? And even Kallimachos and his sons seemed to be in low spirits, especially the elder son, whose name Praxilla didn't remember, and his wife as well. 'I hope Kallisto is not seriously ill', she thought. 'I hope that's not what's wrong. I remember when my cousin's brother-in-law…' Her musings were interrupted by the sound of running feet. They all looked up to see a slave, whom Praxilla recognized as belonging to her nephew Stephanos, gesticulating in an agitated manner, and running towards them. When he reached them and he was asked to speak, he hesitated, looking in Praxilla's direction, and then said, "There's been a killing. The overseers of the sacred rites would like you to stay and talk to them, or at least give me your names and addresses. Just give your names and addresses in your case, I should think."

There was a shocked silence and then someone, Kallimachos, Praxilla thought, asked "What killing? Who was killed?"

The slave hesitated again, again looking towards Praxilla.

"One of the adolescent helpers was found dead," he said eventually.

Kallias jumped up and rushed at him. "Who?" he screamed at the slave "Tell me, which helper is dead?" The slave hesitated again and Kallias started shaking him, demanding to know who had been killed. By the time he revealed that it was Daphne, after more meaningful glances in Praxilla's direction, the news that her niece was dead came as somewhat less of a shock to Praxilla than it might have done otherwise. Which may have been what the slave had intended all along. He told them what he knew about Daphne's death.

Praxilla had never felt close to Daphne, the girl's personality grated on her nerves, but all the same… She was her dead brother's daughter, and she'd seen her grow up, and now she wasn't there any more. She wasn't going to get older, get married… Praxilla had seen too much death in her life to be seriously shaken by Daphne's death, but she felt immensely sad. The girl was like a beautiful flower someone had crushed with a stone. Praxilla's eyes filled with tears. Kallisto put her arms around her. "Oh, my dear, I am so very sorry," she said, hugging Praxilla. "And I thought I had problems…" she added, almost to herself.

The two walked away, heading for Philon's house, where Praxilla had ritual duties to perform, as the dead girl's kinswoman, together with Olympias, lament, wash the body and lay it out.

The others followed behind them, at a distance. Before they started out Kallias, who had calmed down when he heard who the victim was, asked the slave who had killed Daphne. The slave replied that Alexias, the son of Nikias and the priestess Theano had been found with the body, and it was believed that he had killed her.

Kallias burst into laughter. "You can't be serious. That wimp wouldn't kill a frog. He hasn't got the guts, and he wouldn't manage to do it even if he wanted to. He'd run ten stadia rather than kiss a girl, let alone kill her."

"Don't be so flippant," his father admonished him. "A young girl is dead. And you don't know the circumstances; you don't know what may have happened. People can do all sorts of things you don't expect them to when they are under pressure."

Kallias smiled. "You are right I don't know the circumstances. But I'll bet you anything you like, that Alexias didn't kill that girl."

Chapter Seven

Obviously, I don't know the lad, but I can't believe he could have been that stupid, to kill her and then stay around to be found out, however demented with grief or fury or whatever he may have been. Daphne must have been dead for quite a while before Melissa found him with the body, otherwise she would have joined us long before. She was obviously killed with that jagged stone they said they found in the brook. The men who examined the body said that she was hit on the head several times and that she wasn't raped. Neither I nor Theano could go and see, obviously, we can't go near a corpse; now, more than ever, we must not come into contact with death, and become polluted, otherwise we wouldn't be able to perform the rites we must perform for the festival. It was lucky for all of us that Melissa turned to stone from the shock when she found them, she could so easily have rushed to the body instead, and then we would have had a problem. And the goddess must have inspired Kallisto and Eunice to stop the other little fools from rushing down and polluting themselves. I don't know what we would have done, we would have had to exclude them from the rites and the festival and they wouldn't have been able to finish their service. What terrifies me is that if the killer isn't Alexias, or any of Daphne's relatives, who are polluted anyway, and can't come into the sanctuary, it may be someone who will be taking part in the rites, and they would defile the goddess, and the sanctuary and the festival, which would be catastrophic for all of us – and worst of all for the city. So I must find out who killed Daphne and establish that he is really the killer before the festival. It may be Alexias after all; in a way, I suppose, I hope it is, but we have to be sure.

Chapter Eight

"I didn't kill her. You've got to believe me. I just found her. She was dead when I found her. Why should I kill her? I love her." Alexias had been protesting his innocence ever since he was arrested. A gangling youth, his legs disproportionately long for his torso, he was not unpleasing to the eye, with his curly fair hair and green eyes. He was being taken back to the house of the mayor of the nearest village, where he was going to be kept under guard until after the festival; then he would be taken to the city. As they were coming out of the woods Chloe approached Stephanos. "Do you think it might be possible for me to have a word with Alexias?" she asked.

"If you want, I suppose so. I don't see why not."

"I was thinking, on my own, without you and the slaves around."

"Oh, I see. Look, I'm sorry, but that's impossible …he would get away. You couldn't stop him."

"What if he gave me his word of honour that he wouldn't?"

"But you can't believe that he would keep it. He's a murderer. He killed my sister. I can't risk losing him. He'll just run away and flee the country."

"Oh, come on… He's only nineteen. Where would he go? How far would he get?"

"What has age got to do with it? His family are bound to have guest friends abroad. Nothing is easier than to find a boat and slip away."

"I would take full responsibility. And you could place the slaves all around us in a circle, as long as you are all far enough away, so that you can't hear what we are saying. Otherwise he won't be prepared to talk to me freely."

"And what makes you think he'll want to talk to you freely anyway?"

"The fact that I don't think he's the killer?"

"You don't?"

"No, I don't."

Stephanos said nothing for a few seconds; he was staring into the distance as though he were alone. Eventually, he gestured the slaves to move away with the prisoner and said, "I am not going to ask you why, not just now, but perhaps we may be able to discuss this some other time. This is what I suggest. The next few days are not going to be easy for me – for a variety of reasons you can guess; and holding the priestess' son prisoner during the festival, and not being able to come into the sanctuary myself – the whole thing is a nightmare. So I am going to need some help, and maybe we can make a deal – you help me, I help you, and we support each other when we need help?"

"I'm not sure what you mean by 'when we need help'; I am not doing anything that goes against my duties, or against the law."

"Against the law? Why should I want you to do anything against the law? Or against your duties, come to that?"

"I don't know, do I? I don't know you. For all I know you may be Daphne's killer."

Stephanos seemed stunned by her aggression; he looked at her and, after a few seconds, said, "I can assure you that I did not kill my sister. But even if I had, I can't imagine why you should think I would need your help to cover up my evil deed."

Chloe focussed on Stephanos for the first time since he had

62

appeared on the scene. She had seen him before, of course, even spoken to him, but she had never paid him much attention – just another rich relative, just another magistrate. He was a tall good looking man in his mid-thirties with brown hair and blue eyes, but his face at the moment looked rigid, like carved Pentelic marble. "I'm sorry," she said eventually.

"No, I don't think you are, but never mind about that. Do tell me why you think I may be the murderer, when we have the culprit here, caught red-handed?"

"Because I told you, I am not at all sure that Alexias did it."

"And why is that, may I ask?"

"Well, it's a sort of feeling that's made up of a lot of little things, and I cannot put my finger on all of them. But one thing that I do know worries me is this, if he killed her, why did he stay around to be found out? He would have had to have killed her quite some time before Melissa found them, otherwise Daphne would have joined us long before."

"Not if she had been waiting for him."

"But she knew that she would have been in a lot of trouble if she wasn't there at the end of the Hunt."

"She wouldn't have cared if they were going to elope."

"No…" Chloe thought about it, and repeated, "No, I don't think that's very likely, that they were going to elope. Believe me, I did know Daphne, and it really isn't very likely. But I'll ask him anyway."

"And you really think he's going to tell you the truth?"

"He doesn't know there is any reason not to tell me the truth about this."

"Whatever he tells you, the fact is that he is the only one covered in blood. There would have been a lot of blood when the killer broke Daphne's head, and some of it would have got on to the killer's clothes. And no one else except Alexias had blood on their clothes."

"We don't know that, maybe the killer isn't one of the people we saw afterwards; or maybe whoever did it cleaned themselves up and changed. They could have hidden a bundle of clothes anywhere if they knew their way around the woods."

"Are you saying that the murder was premeditated?"

"I don't know. If that's what happened it must have been. But I am not sure that the killer would necessarily have been drenched in blood. If someone came up from behind as she was sitting on the ground and they hit her on the head, would they have got blood on their clothes?"

"I don't know, but she wouldn't have just sat there if someone was coming at her from behind. Or would she? I suppose she would have done if it was her lover."

"Or her brother."

"Or her subpriestess."

Chloe was incensed. How dare he? "That's totally ridiculous. How could you possibly think such a thing? It's preposterous. Why should I want to kill Daphne? I haven't got any reason to kill her."

"That we know of. And anyway, it's obvious that you disliked her."

"Oh come on. If I killed everyone I disliked Daphne wouldn't have been first on my list. I know you know that it's ridiculous. You are just trying to divert my attention away from you. And anyway, when would I have been able to do it? I was with other people all the time …well, almost all the time. I was moving from group to group."

"So was I; almost all the time." After a short silence he went on. "You are so certain of yourself, aren't you? You are certain Alexias didn't kill Daphne, and you are certain that I am a serious suspect."

"I didn't say I was certain about anything, I just have doubts about the obvious solution."

"And so you chose the less obvious one of assuming it was me – that it could have been me. Or is it less obvious?"

"Look, I don't know you. Why shouldn't I think you are a serious suspect?"

"For a start, where is my motive?"

"And where is Alexias' motive?"

"I don't know, but he keeps telling us he loves her, so I think you'll find that he does have one. I really cannot understand why you think I would kill her. What did I have to gain?"

"Well, you didn't like her, and you hated her mother. And you obviously think disliking someone is a credible motive for killing them."

"I see. And why do you think I snapped suddenly after all these years?"

"Maybe you were in the woods and you saw her sitting there alone, and it brought it all home."

"While I was wandering idly around the woods instead of performing the duties I was supposed to perform?"

"Maybe it was premeditated; maybe you thought that she would soon be getting married, and you would have to give her a big dowry or lose face, and now you won't have to."

He gave a dry laugh. "So basically I killed my sister to save myself some money. I see…"

"You just find all this very amusing, don't you? You think you are safe, and that no one is going to listen to me, so it amuses you to play with me."

"I can assure you, amusing is the last thing I find this conversation."

"You obviously think that no one in your position and with

your respectability and your money is going to be suspected of such a horrible thing."

"If you mean that people will think that a man who has led an unblemished life for thirty-four years is less likely to have suddenly committed a terrible crime, then you are right, I do think that." He paused, and then went on. "And I am not going to continue this ridiculous conversation. Forget about the deal. You can talk to Alexias in private, provided he gives his word of honour, and you take full responsibility, and we stand around you in a circle …far away, but in a circle." He turned his back on her and went to order the slaves to bring the prisoner over.

After Alexias and Chloe had given solemn undertakings of good faith and responsibility the others withdrew some distance away. Chloe sat on the ground. Alexias was about to join her, but she stopped him. "Don't come too near me; whether or not you are the killer, you are covered in Daphne's blood, and I don't want to risk you polluting me." After a short silence she continued. "What were you doing in the wood with Daphne? According to your mother you are still doing your ephebic service, patrolling the frontier."

"Yes, I am. I'm stationed at Rhamnous. I got a lift in an oxcart last night."

"I didn't think you could get off duty any time you felt like it. Things must have changed a lot since my brother did his service, if you can get off like that any time you want."

"They don't know I'm gone. We are supposed to do mountain training, going to ground on our own; I slipped off and my mates are covering for me."

"So now they are going to be in trouble too."

"No, they won't. You don't think I'm going to admit that they knew and covered up for me, do you? What sort of person do you think I am?"

"I don't know, do I? All I've seen so far is that you put your friends at risk of serious trouble because you wanted to do what you wanted to do, and you wouldn't let anything stop you."

"But I didn't do it on purpose. I just never thought anything would go wrong. How was I to know what was going to happen?" He stopped. "Anyway nothing matters any more. I may as well be dead... But I didn't kill her. I didn't. I love her. That's why I came; that's why I took the risk."

"Why?"

"She sent me a message to come and see her immediately."

"And you came."

"I told you. I love her. Loved her. I would have done anything she asked."

"And did you find out why she summoned you?"

"I saw her very briefly last night and we arranged to meet in the woods today, but when I got there she was dead."

"Why had she summoned you so urgently?"

Alexias blushed. He looked at his feet and he kicked some stones down the slope. "I'm sorry. I can't tell you that. It's private. It's between Daphne and me."

"Daphne's dead, and the chances are you are going to be convicted of her murder. So if you've got a story that makes sense, you'd better tell it, starting with me."

"But I can't. I can't talk about things like that. Not to a woman anyway."

"Well, in that case I'll tell you what she wanted. She wanted to let you know that she was pregnant and you had to get married."

The young man stopped in his tracks. "How did you know that?" he said. "No one was supposed to know. She only told me last night."

"Never mind about that. Just tell me, who else knew you

were meeting her there?"

"No one."

"How do you know that?"

"Well, I suppose Daphne could have said something to someone, but why should she?"

"Could someone have overheard your conversation last night? Where did you meet?"

"In the back outer porch of the amphipoleion. But no one saw us, and Daphne sneaked out of the room she shared with the other helpers without them knowing, she'd given them drugged wine to drink, and she gave some to the Spartan priestess as well, just to be on the safe side. So the girls didn't know she'd left the room, and there was no one else about. You don't think the slaves patrol the building to keep order when you aren't there, do you?"

"Wasn't she worried that I might see you?"

"No, she'd guessed my mother would call you away to go over things, and that it would take a long time. I've often told her how much my mother always frets and keeps people awake at night, and she thought she was bound to do that the night before the Sacred Hunt, so she waited until she saw you leave before coming out."

"I see… She had everything worked out very carefully."

"Anyway, that's when we arranged to meet this morning, in our special secret place."

"Is that where you used to meet?"

"Well, that's where we went the one time that, you know…"

"You mean you only had sex with her once? When was that?"

Alexias was red with embarrassment, which he turned to aggression… "What is it to you? Why do you ask all these questions?"

68

"Just answer me, Alexias."

"Why should I?"

"Because I say so, and because I work with your mother, and because Stephanos arranged for me to question you."

"What do I care?"

"Well, you should care, if you are really innocent, and you want to try to save your skin. It's your only chance at the moment."

"What do you mean?"

"Never mind what I mean. Just answer the question."

"All right, yes, it was only once, just over a month ago. I've admired her for a very long time, of course, and she knew it, but…"

"I suppose someone could have followed Daphne to the place you were supposed to meet," Chloe interrupted him.

"But why should they? And how would they know we were meeting?"

"Maybe they didn't, I don't know, Alexias, this is what I am trying to find out. Obviously, someone wanted to kill her, so they may well have followed her, hoping to catch her alone, as they did."

"It's all my fault. If I had got there earlier, if I hadn't been so late… I'll never forgive myself for this."

"Why were you late?"

"I had a row with my father, we blew up at each other and I was too enraged to go and meet Daphne in that state."

"What was the row about?"

Alexias hesitated.

"You told him about Daphne, didn't you?"

"Yes, I did. I suppose you would have found out anyway. I sent his personal slave to tell him that I was here and to come and see me because it was a matter of life and death, and he came."

"And what happened when you told him?"

"I told you, he went into a rage, shouting and screaming, I'm surprised they didn't hear us all over the woods. He said that I was a bloody fool, that Daphne was a tart and the daughter of a tart. And that I would marry her over his dead body. That he would disown me."

"I am surprised he took it that badly. It wouldn't have been such a bad match, surely. Her family is good, and very, very rich, and my guess is she would have got an extremely good dowry."

"It's not her family as such, more her mother being, well, you know, not very proper. And that Daphne had slept with me. And he said I was far too young to get married. Plus, he had always hoped I'd marry my cousin Melissa who is an epikleros. But the main thing was that I am too young, and Daphne wasn't a virtuous virgin."

"But it was you who was responsible for that."

"I know, but he …well, he said I couldn't possibly know that, and how did I know the child was mine anyway?"

"And what did you say?"

"I told him that he was disgusting even to think such a thing, and then I said that I loved Daphne, and that I was going to marry her, whatever. I didn't really believe he would disown me. I am his only son, if he disowned me his household would come to an end, and no one wants that, that's why people adopt sons. He wouldn't do it."

"You are probably right; and if you are, that gives your father a very good motive for killing Daphne."

Alexias looked astounded. "That's ridiculous," he said indignantly. "You can't be serious. My father would never kill anyone."

"I thought he already had; wasn't he a general and,

70

according to your mother, a war hero?"

"But that's totally different, that's war. Killing your enemies in battle is totally different. As a woman, you wouldn't understand, but believe me…"

"Let's not go into that." Chloe interrupted him brusquely. "Tell me, then, who do you think killed Daphne, if it wasn't you, and it wasn't your father? Who else would want to kill her?"

"I don't know. Her family hated her, especially her older brother, Stephanos… Now he comes over high and mighty, pretending he cares that she's dead and wanting to prosecute me, but he made her life a misery. She told me. And her mother wasn't much better, if you want the truth."

"That's ridiculous. Olympias adored Daphne, she was the centre of her world."

"That's what everyone thinks. But the way she treated Daphne over the business with that old pervert who wants to marry her, I wouldn't be so sure myself. She's probably jealous."

"What old pervert? What are you talking about?"

"Andreas, the son of Archias, from Marathon; he wants to marry Olympias, and Daphne was dead against it, and she told her mother that Andreas had made sexual advances to her. Her mother didn't believe her, in fact, she got very angry and then she went and told him, Andreas, and he was really rude to Daphne. He threatened her."

"And was it true? Had he made sexual advances to her?"

"Of course it was true. How dare you suggest that Daphne would tell lies? Come to think of it, maybe it was the old pervert who killed her, because of what she said; he was probably afraid that in the end she would manage to convince her mother not to marry him. And…"

"I am sorry that will have to be all for now," Stephanos' voice cut into Alexias' words. "We are coming to get him." They

71

came over and the slaves grabbed Alexias in a tight hold and marched him down the slope towards the village.

Chapter Nine

Alexias didn't kill her. I'm sure of that. Stephanos, I'm not so sure. Or am I? Maybe I just want to think he might have done it. And not just because he's polluted and excluded from the sanctuary anyway, which would make our life easier; he's one of them, one of the men who have power and run things. And he has this unbreakable self-confidence.

But do I really believe he killed Daphne?

I'll try to think this through, one step at a time.

It can't have been a stranger, because she wasn't raped. Why should a stranger want to kill her otherwise? If she had been raped it would have made sense, killing her to stop her raising the alarm. Unless he was mad. I suppose it could have been a madman, wandering in the woods, stumbling on her by accident. But if a madman was wandering around in the woods someone would have seen him, wouldn't they?

What else would make a stranger want to kill her? I guess she might have seen something she wasn't supposed to, something secret that happened while everyone was meant to be at the Hunt, around the clearing, with the bears hunting further up the slope. Maybe she was killed to stop her from telling what she saw? But what could she possibly have seen that was worth the risk of killing her?

And another thing that's worrying me. I never thought that Daphne was romantic, or sentimental. I always saw her as cold and calculating, out for the main chance. Now Alexias is a good enough catch, but she could have done so much better for herself. I can't believe that she would have risked everything for love. Have I been wrong all along?

Chapter Ten

Mego had accompanied Theano and her husband Nikias to the village, which was the centre of the deme (a territorial district, Chloe had explained to Mego) called Philaidai. Theano's daughter Kleopatra was already there, with her husband Phanes. They tried to comfort Theano, but she just went on crying and bewailing her fate. When she saw Alexias arriving with Stephanos and the guards she made to rush and throw herself at him and Nikias had to restrain her, to stop her from polluting herself.

"What have you done?" she cried. "How could you do such a thing? You've ruined us… Why did you do it? What are we going to do now?"

Alexias stopped and said, in an even voice, "I didn't do it. It wasn't me." It was as though his mother's hysteria had sucked up his own, and left him calm and composed.

"You asked me to have her back here as a helper, and I did. I should never have listened to you," Theano continued, as Nikias pushed her onto Chloe and followed Alexias and his guards inside.

Stephanos went into the mayor's house, handed over Alexias to the mayor's custody, and then left. He had been staying in the sanctuary, because he was one of the five overseers of the sacred rites involved with the arrangements at Brauron before the festival – the other five were coming with the procession from the city which began the festival. But now that he was polluted by Daphne's death he could not return there, so he was going to stay at the house of Daphne's maternal grandfather, Philon. He had to be there anyway, for, as Daphne's closest adult male relative and guardian he had to organize and conduct her funeral. Chloe had instructed Bakchis to send his things on to Philon's house and to make sure that the slaves who took them had purified themselves before they returned to the sanctuary. Daphne's mother and aunt had washed her body and anointed it with perfume, clothed and adorned it with jewellery, and then laid it out on a couch; friends and neighbours would be going to visit all day and into the night, while the women of the family would be lamenting and tearing their hair – this was the rite called prothesis. The funeral had to take place on the day after this prothesis, before sunrise. All this Chloe had explained to Mego, because she knew that the Spartans arranged things a bit differently from most Greeks when it came to the death ritual, only she wasn't quite sure how.

After Nikias had followed the others into the mayor's house, Chloe dragged Theano away with Mego's help. When they were out of earshot she turned on her. "Are you completely crazy? Do you think it is going to help Alexias having his own mother declaring in public that he's guilty?"

Theano stopped trying to free herself from Chloe's grasp and stood still, staring at Chloe in confusion. "What are you talking about?" she asked. "They told me everyone knows he's guilty. We found him with her body. And I knew he was in love with her."

"That wasn't a reason for him to kill her."

"But we found him with the body, we all saw him. Anyway, if she was pregnant as you said… They are going to say that he made her pregnant and then he didn't want to marry her and she was going to make trouble, and that's why he killed her."

76

"But he did want to marry her. He loved her."

"Yes, but his father wouldn't have let him – well, not easily, anyway. He would have had a struggle on his hands, and they are going to say he didn't want to bother after all."

"But we can't even be sure that Alexias made her pregnant. They apparently only slept together once, and that wasn't much more than just over a month ago. I suspect Daphne's pregnancy was further along than that."

"That's even worse. They are going to say that she was pregnant by someone else, and he killed her out of jealousy."

Chloe's resources of tact were now exhausted, and she didn't try to hide her irritation. "Can't you just forget for a moment what 'they' are going to say, and think about what you think? Do you really think your son killed Daphne? And if you don't know, shouldn't you keep your mouth shut?"

"Why are you asking me this? What's it to you? Leave me alone. It's none of your business."

"I'm asking you and telling you because I am not sure that Alexias is guilty."

"What makes you say that? And what is it to you?"

"You mean besides my innate sense of justice? But of course you wouldn't understand that, so let's pretend I am being ironic, and let me tell you what's in it for me and for everyone else, which is obvious to everyone except you, though, to be fair, I suppose you are in shock. If the killer isn't Alexias, or any of Daphne's relatives, who can't come into the sanctuary because they are polluted anyway, it could be someone who is going to take part in the rites in the festival; and so he will defile the goddess, and the sanctuary and the festival. And you know the consequences of that."

"He or she," Mego said. "The killer could have been a woman."

"Yes, I'm sure you are right," Chloe admitted. "We can't exclude a woman killer."

"So what are we going to do?" Theano's question was meant as a despondent sigh, but Chloe responded as though it had been a request for her opinion.

"We can't cancel the festival obviously; and even if that had been possible, the killer could still come and pollute the sanctuary anyway. There is only one thing we can do; we can try to work out who the killer is, if it wasn't Alexias. And before you ask, no, I don't know how we are going to do that, but I know we've got to try." After a short silence she continued. "But first we must go back to the sanctuary and make sure that everything is as normal as it could be in the circumstances, and also prepare for the purification of the sacred grove. I am sorry, Theano, but you have to pull yourself together. We all must. We must keep our head and do the best we can. The festival begins in four days' time."

"And of course I'll help in whatever way I can and I am allowed to," Mego offered.

"Thank you, that's extremely kind of you," Chloe said. Theano said nothing, but she did follow Chloe's instructions. Before they left the village they purified themselves with spring water, since for the purposes of ritual purity it was safer to assume that Alexias was the killer, and so purify themselves as though they had been talking to, and looking at, a murderer.

When they got back they found the sanctuary in chaos. It was difficult to know where to start and what to do. Chloe instructed Bakchis to get the other slaves back to work, and start putting together the stuff needed for the purification of the sacred grove. She then told Theano to snap out of it and go to talk to the four overseers of the sacred rites who remained in the sanctuary; things needed to be worked out. "I must go and organize the bears," she said to Mego. "You are welcome to join me." They walked together in the direction of the gymnasium. "In normal circumstances," Chloe said, "they would be doing gymnastic exercises just now, to loosen them up for the rehearsal of the dances. But now..." She lifted her arms in a gesture of resignation. "I expect they were really shaken... Such a violent death, so near them, and someone so close... Obviously, they are used to death from disease and war, but this is something else."

They found the bears in a small olive grove not far from the gymnasium; they were lying about in various poses of dejection, apparently barely moving. Anthea, Electra, and Helena were sitting around looking shocked and at the same time excited. "There is nothing we can do with them," Anthea said when she saw Chloe. "They are all in a very funny mood, we can't even talk to them. I'm sorry, but we've just given up."

"Yes, I know, I wasn't expecting anything else. I have to go to a meeting in a moment, and then Theano and I will have to purify the sacred wood, so I'm afraid I'll have to leave you to cope all on your own for quite some time. I suggest that we give up on the idea of getting them to do any work today. I think you should all go to the beach and have a nice long swim. It's good exercise, and they'll let off tension. Tomorrow we'll start the day with another swim and then try to work as normal and catch up as much as we can."

"Okay, we'll do that, then," Anthea replied.

"Ahm," Electra spoke hesitantly. "There is one problem. I don't think that Melissa will want to come swimming. She's in a bad way. Really devastated. Daphne's death would have been bad enough, she had a crush on her, as we all know, but finding her dead like that, and with her own cousin. It must have been terrible, poor child. She looks crushed."

"I'm sorry, but she'll have to go swimming just like

everyone else. It's been a terrible shock for all of them, and all of us, come to that; I realize it's worse for Melissa, but Kallisto also had a difficult time, she had to carry the responsibility of the Hunt, and then this happened. And I'm sure she hasn't been complaining."

"No, of course not, but then Kallisto is special…"

"Ooohh." Anthea and Helena mocked Electra.

"I'm sorry, but that's that," Chloe said firmly. "I am not going to have one little girl under my feet with all that's going on. They all have to learn to cope. Especially a self-important little madam like Melissa." Mego had eventually repeated to her the conversation she had overheard on the way to the Sacred Hunt, and Chloe had had no difficulty in identifying Melissa as the 'blackmailer' and Kallisto as the victim. So she did not feel inclined to do Melissa any favours just now.

"To be fair, this time…"

"Yes, I know, but that's that."

When Anthea, Electra and Helena went to tell the girls of the new plan some at least got excited and started jumping about, miraculously recovering their energy. Melissa remained subdued, but to the helpers' surprise she didn't object to the expedition. She just passively followed the others without saying anything.

"She's totally crushed, poor thing; she's like a different person," Electra commented, as they all started walking to the beach.

"About time too, that she was a different person," laughed Anthea.

"Speaking of different people," Helena said, "Would you ever have thought that Alexias would have killed someone?"

"Well, he's being trained to kill, isn't he?" Electra pointed out.

"But that's totally different," Helena objected. "That's training for war to fight for his country."

"Is it really different?"

"Oh, come on Electra," Anthea intervened. "It is totally different, and you know it. Every man fights for his country, but they don't go on and murder the people they dislike."

"I don't think Alexias killed Daphne because he disliked her. The other way round I would have thought." Helena said.

"What do you mean?"

"Well, she was apparently pregnant, and I saw Alexias ogling her at a wedding months ago."

"Really? And what did she do?"

"At the time I didn't think she was interested, but obviously, she must have been, otherwise she wouldn't have got pregnant." They all laughed. "It's funny, you know," Helena mused "Daphne is the last person I would have expected to risk everything for love. We all know what she was like, and Alexias is all right, but not really all that much of a catch, not compared to what she could have got instead."

"She obviously loved him. Anyone can fall in love," Electra protested.

"You are such an innocent," Anthea patted her arm affectionately. "We need to do something about that if you are going to bring a certain young gentleman where you want him."

"Oh, Anthea," Electra sighed, "It's no use. It's hopeless."

"No, you mustn't say that. There may be all sorts of reasons why your father and your cousin came to the Hunt together. And in any case, you never know, you may manage to work something out, you and Kallias between you."

Electra started crying. "There is no me and Kallias between us. He's not interested in me."

"But… I thought you said… I know you said at the Hunt

that he wasn't beating a path to your door, but that's because you were upset about seeing your father with your cousin; I mean, you wouldn't expect Kallias to be beating a path to your door at this stage, would you? But you did say he had been looking at you in a certain way every time he had the chance, when you saw each other, and that he was trying to make opportunities for you to bump into each other when no one was around, though he hadn't managed it yet."

"Yes, that's what I'd thought… But obviously I was wrong. I was imagining it. What would I know? It was obviously just wishful thinking. He certainly cut me dead when we came face to face during the Hunt, when I went for a short walk just before the bears came back with the stag."

"Oh, Electra, I am so sorry. Why didn't you say?"

"I might have done, but then the bears came back, and then there was the hassle of getting all the girls packed up and going, and then, of course, we discovered Daphne had been killed. And I know my little problem is nothing compared to that."

"But it's important to you. Just because something big happens, it doesn't mean we must all measure ourselves against it all the time. Problems are problems."

"I wish I were dead…"

"I don't know why you bother with all that stuff," Helena cut into the conversation. "Glances across the courtyard, and love from afar… All it does is make you miserable. That's why I am perfectly happy to marry the man my father chose for me."

"But you don't love him."

"I don't know what you mean by love, Electra. How can you love a man you hardly know, like you do Kallias? You are attracted by his beauty, but is that really what love is? I don't know, do you? This man I'm supposed to marry, he's a nice boy, he's not bad looking, and his father is a friend of my father's, so I know all about him... What is it that you think I am missing? Maybe you like yearning for things. I'm not like that."

"I bet," Anthea said, "that you wouldn't have felt the same if it had been your father's friend, rather than his son, that your father had wanted you to marry, like some fathers do."

"Perhaps, perhaps not. I don't know. But for me, the main thing is to be mistress of your own house, have an agreeable husband, and ideally have sons you bring up to help you do what you want to do, since we need a man to act for us in so many things. So why bother with all this yearning from afar and be miserable?"

"I wouldn't be miserable if Kallias loved me."

"Yes, you would, because you would still be an epikleros and his father still wouldn't let him be adopted by your father."

"Maybe, but if everything was unproblematic, like with Anthea and Agias, then I would have been happy. They are going to get married, and they did fall in love and they are happy."

"And how exactly do you think Agias is different from the sort of man her father would have chosen?"

"Don't be silly, that's not the point. The point is that she chose him herself." Then, in a different tone, looking behind Anthea and Helena, "What do you think you are doing? Stop it this instant." The other two turned around to see who was doing what this time; a tall slim little girl was tickling a much smaller one who was shrieking for help and trying to get away.

"Eunice! Stop it this instant!" Anthea shouted, as she rushed to grab the bigger girl. "Aren't you ashamed of yourself, attacking someone younger and smaller than you? Haven't you learnt anything all this time?"

"She started it," Eunice cried indignantly. "Zoe and her friend Thekla, they grabbed me from behind and started it, and then Thekla ran away."

"That's enough. Never mind who started it. You aren't supposed to do that, and you know it."

"But that's not fair. If you say it doesn't matter who started it you are automatically favouring the aggressor. Did you hear that, Kallisto?" Eunice said to her friend, who was running in their direction. "There they go again. It doesn't matter if you've been attacked; you are not supposed to do anything about it."

"Never mind them, Eunice," Kallisto said. "They are not worth getting upset about." She didn't really believe that, not as far as Electra was concerned at least, but you have to show loyalty to your friends.

"No, you are right." Eunice threw her head back like a thoroughbred colt, shaking her hair, so that it flew behind her, and stared at the helpers. "They are just silly girls who don't know how to think for themselves, so they have simple recipes for all situations." She flounced off, arm in arm with Kallisto, leaving the older girls torn between fury and amusement.

Chapter Eleven

Chloe had left Mego at the amphipoleion and gone to make sure that the preparations necessary for the purification of the wood were under way. She inspected the piglet that had been selected for the sacrifice and she found it satisfactory. It would be killed in the wood and its blood would be spilled over the ground in the clearing, at the place where Daphne's body was found, and in other places all over, then its dead body would be carried around the perimeter of the wood, that is, around the bottom of the wooded hill, for Artemis' sacred grove covered the whole hill.

Afterwards, she picked up Mego and they both went to the house of the priestess. In front of the entrance Mego noticed an inscribed stone slab crowned by a pediment. She stopped to read it aloud.

We honour Iphigeneia
our first priestess,
sacrificed to the goddess
by her father, Agamemnon,
in return for good winds,
for sailing to Troy,
to avenge the honour of Helen's husband,
fair Menelaos, brother of Agamemnon.
The goddess snatched her from the altar,
leaving a deer in her place,
so the deer was sacrificed
and Iphigeneia lived

to become a virgin priestess
among barbarians,
conducting human sacrifice,
until the goddess let her go free,
and sent her here to Brauron,
to become our first priestess.

"So this is to remind Theano, day in day out, what she has to live up to," Mego commented when she finished reading.

"She's buried over there, you know, Iphigeneia," Chloe told her, pointing to an area of higher ground a bit south of the temple.

Inside the house they were met by Bakchis and taken to Theano's private quarters. "I asked Mego to join us," Chloe told the priestess. "Another pair of eyes and ears" – 'other than mine, that is', she thought; Theano didn't seem able to function, let alone make any major contributions. But of course she had to be involved. Not that they managed to get very far, the three of them. They thrashed out the potential murder suspects, but they didn't know enough about them to assess the likelihood of their guilt or innocence; and they didn't know who else might have had a reason to kill Daphne, or if it had been a stranger. They discussed Alexias, Stephanos, Nikias and Andreas – rather, Chloe and Mego did, with Theano only contributing feeble protests at the idea that her husband could have been the killer. In fact Chloe agreed with her; she thought it was extremely unlikely that Nikias had murdered Daphne to protect his son. "He's too calculating a person to kill her before he had exhausted all other avenues with Alexias," she said.

Mego didn't consider Stephanos a serious suspect either; she poured scorn on the idea that he had a motive. "If he killed Daphne because he didn't like her, and hated her mother, why would he have waited until now?" she asked. "He would have done it years ago, while the wound was still fresh. And why not kill Olympias herself? And the idea that he killed her to avoid giving her a dowry without losing face …a man as rich as you tell me this Stephanos is would have to be a raving lunatic to do that; any man, but one as rich as that even more."

"But these are men hardened to killing, fighting wars made them so, surely," Chloe objected. "Taking a life can't mean that much to them."

"No, you don't understand," Mego told her. "In their eyes killing in battle is totally different. Believe me, it is."

Chloe was silent for a few seconds. Then she said "Right… I'll take your word for it on this. At least for the time being. Let's move on. Alexias claimed that Andreas, the son of Archias, from Marathon, wants to marry Olympias, and had a motive to kill Daphne." She told them the story Alexias had told her. "What do we think of that?"

Andreas himself was an unknown quantity, but the story Daphne had fed Alexias did not ring true to the three women. "It sounds to me as though Daphne made it all up to drive a wedge between her mother and Andreas, but Olympias being no fool and, from what everyone is telling me, a master of manipulation herself, didn't fall for it." This was Mego's verdict. "I don't see what this Andreas would have to fear from Daphne, or gain from her death. Certainly nothing worth taking a risk for."

"So that's that then," Theano said. "We are back where we started."

"Not necessarily," Mego said. "We decided that Alexias is almost certainly not the killer." Mego had agreed with Chloe's reading of the situation. Theano, of course, wanted to believe they were right, but she didn't know if a court would be convinced, not unless the real murderer was found.

"Anyway, we haven't considered all possibilities," Chloe added. "What about her mother? We haven't considered Daphne's mother." She turned to Mego. "Do you think Olympias is out of the running?"

"All I can tell you is that after I joined their party she wasn't out of sight for long enough to do it. Before that obviously I don't know – or after, come to that, though Daphne was probably dead by then; but there was plenty of time before I went over for her to have found Daphne in the woods and killed her."

Theano was indignant. "How can you be so horrible and heartless, both of you? She's her mother. Why should she kill her own daughter?"

"We don't know, do we?" Chloe replied. "She may have had her reasons. Medea had her reasons when she killed her children, and so did plenty of other women, Greek women, so don't give me all that rubbish about Medea being a barbarian. Including our very own Athenian princess, Prokne."

"That's not a story I know," Mego remarked.

"You may know other versions of it, with other names. But our local story basically goes like this.

There was an Athenian king who had two daughters, Prokne and Philomela, and he gave Prokne in marriage to a man called Tereus, who some say was a Thracian, but others say he was a Greek from Phokis. Tereus and Prokne had a son called Itys, but then Tereus fell in love with his wife's sister, Philomela. The details vary in the different stories, but anyway, depending on who you believe, he either raped Philomela, or he deceived her and seduced her having lied to her that her sister was dead. He then cut out her tongue, so that she couldn't tell anyone what he had done. But Philomela wove her story into a robe and sent it to Prokne; Prokne sought out her sister, found her, and then killed her son Itys, boiled him, and served him up to Tereus to eat. When Tereus realized what Prokne had done he went after the two sisters with an axe, but they prayed to the gods, and the gods turned all three into birds: Prokne became a nightingale, Philomela a swallow and Tereus a hoopoe."

"Not a pretty story."

"No. It's not meant to be. It's no use making up stories that just tell people what they want to hear; we've got to teach them the realities as well…"

"The realities being that all women are bad, or can turn bad and so can't be trusted," Theano said sharply.

"We've had this discussion before, Theano," Chloe said impatiently. "And I told you, myths are more complex than that. When I was first taught these stories I thought, typical stories made up by men against women. And it's true, that's one of the things these stories say, that women can turn bad, and that when they do they will use the weapons of the weak, which are deceitful and violent, and hurt men where they are vulnerable to women, in the family, by killing their sons. But that's not the whole story. It's a warning to men as well, they are saying that if men abuse their power it will be their own fault if there is disaster; the women do wrong and they are bad women, but they do it because the men abused them. Even Medea. So it's a warning to men: don't abuse your power over women, or else you'll suffer as well."

"This is fascinating, I'm sure, but we've got more urgent things to discuss just now, I would have thought." Theano was openly patronizing, sounding more like her usual self, Chloe thought. "Yes, fine, let's go back to the matter at hand," she replied.

"Olympias' husband is dead, I understand," Mego said. "So if she did kill her daughter, whatever her reason, it wasn't to punish the father, like Medea and this Prokne."

"And the story goes that she had other ways of punishing him if he ever got out of line, not that he did, apparently; if there was abuse of power in that marriage it went the other way. She had him wrapped up around her little finger – or so they say."

"In any case," Theano said, "killing a daughter is not the same punishment for a father as killing a son."

"No doubt, but it is in any case irrelevant."

"What other reason could she possibly have had?"

"Actually, Alexias seemed to think that Olympias was jealous of Daphne because of Andreas, but I don't really believe that a mother could kill her own daughter for such a reason, even if the rest of what Alexias told me had been true, and we all agreed it was fantasies fed him by Daphne for her own reasons."

"Unless…" Mego mused "she hit out at Daphne in anger, and then it was too late to stop."

"Yes, I suppose that's not impossible, but I don't know…" Chloe said.

"There is someone else who definitely did have a motive," Theano offered. "Daphne had been making Electra's life a misery; I understand that you saw that for yourself, Mego, didn't you?"

'Ah …ah… So someone is giving detailed reports to Theano about everything that's going on', Chloe thought. 'I hadn't realized that; she had been very careful until now not to reveal anything she wasn't supposed to know, but now that she's under pressure she made a slip in an unguarded moment. Not that I have anything to hide, but it goes to show what she's like. I wonder who her spy is. Bakchis is of course an obvious possibility, but she doesn't like Theano. On the other hand, liking isn't the point, is it? Bakchis is, after all, a slave and she wouldn't have much choice.'

"Yes, but …surely…" Mego was answering in the

meantime. "You don't kill for something like that."

"Don't you? I should think it all depends. If it's eating into you, destroying your self-esteem, maybe you do. And Daphne was pushing all the right buttons with Electra."

"I don't know… It doesn't ring true somehow, not for me," Mego answered.

"Our problem," Chloe sighed, "is that we don't know anything for certain. We don't even know enough about Daphne. We need to find out more. About Daphne, her family, her friends, their enemies…"

"And how are we going to do that?"

"Well, we could always ask at her grandfather's house." Chloe replied. "I bet there are lots of things the slaves there could tell us, especially the ones who came from the city with Olympias and Daphne."

"Two problems with that," Theano suddenly said. "One, none of us can go to her grandfather's house, because it's polluted. And two, what makes you think they would let us interrogate the slaves even if we could have gone?"

"I know, we would have to play it by ear, maybe do it in secret, offer some bribes." Chloe explained to Mego that even if they hadn't been priestesses they couldn't have gone to Daphne's prothesis, because Athenian law about funerals said that women under sixty were only allowed to go to a prothesis or a funeral if they were close kin to the dead person. Mego thought that was a bit weird, but she said nothing.

The three priestesses thought about the problem in silence for a bit, then Theano said, "Actually, if we could work out some sort of plan, some instructions that wouldn't be too difficult to follow and adapt to the circumstances, we could send my daughter's husband Phanes to Daphne's prothesis."

"And hope for the best," Chloe added.

"Do you have any better ideas?" Theano snapped.

Chloe didn't bother to confirm that she hadn't. And it had been unkind of her to hint at the limitations of Phanes' competence. After all, she didn't really know the man, she was only going by what Theano had let slip when she was especially annoyed with her daughter. And given Theano's trustworthiness, Phanes could be a genius, for all Chloe could know. "Will he be prepared to go?" she asked.

"He'll have to go whether he likes it or not," Theano said. "If it can help save Alexias, he'll just have to do whatever we tell him."

"I don't see how we can manage to devise a plan that will get him to question the slaves. And that's true for anyone else as well, not just Phanes," Chloe hastened to add.

"Maybe we should put our trust in the goddess." This was the first religious thing Mego had heard Theano say in private conversation, and it felt more like an acknowledgment of powerlessness than a realistic hope that Artemis was going to give them a helping hand. Anyway, Theano had started writing a letter summoning her son-in-law, who had gone to visit a friend along the coast, and explaining what would be required of him, when there was a knock on the door and Bakchis came in.

"I did ask not to be interrupted," Theano said sternly.

"I know, and I am very sorry, but your brother is here and he insists on seeing you. He won't take no for an answer."

"Indeed I will not." A man came into the room without waiting. He was much younger than Theano, in his early thirties, tall and very good looking, with the same blond hair and blue eyes as his sister. "What is this, keeping me waiting outside? Since when do I have to wait to see you?" He glared at Theano.

"This is my brother Leon," Theano explained to Mego. "He lives in the deme of Steiria, down the road." To Leon she said,

"This is not a good time. We have major problems on all fronts."

"I know. I was out riding and I heard, so I've come to find out what's going on."

"What's going on is that one of our adolescent helpers has been killed, and my son is accused of her murder."

Leon didn't seem to pay much attention to the news of his nephew's plight. "Is it true that the dead girl is Philon's granddaughter Daphne?" he asked.

"Yes, do you know her?"

"I may have seen her in some wedding or other, I'm not sure." Then, perhaps because he realized that some reaction concerning Alexias was expected of him, he got around to asking, "But why do they think Alexias killed her?"

"He was found with the body. And he had been her lover, and she was pregnant."

"What??" Leon seemed stunned. "Are you sure that Alexias was her lover?"

"Yes. Of course I'm sure. You don't think I would get something like that wrong, do you? Look, it's a long story and this is not the time."

"When did all this happen?"

"This morning, during the Sacred Hunt."

"Do they know when exactly she was killed? What…"

"Listen," Chloe interrupted him, "she told you, we haven't got the time to sit around and answer questions just now. So, if you don't mind, we've got urgent business to discuss. This is a council of priestesses you interrupted."

"What do you mean council of priestesses? She's not a priestess," he said pointing at Mego. "I've never seen her before."

"I am the priestess of Artemis Orthia at Sparta." Mego spoke in an icy voice.

"So? You've got no jurisdiction here."

"I may not have what you call jurisdiction, but I most certainly have ritual competence, which is the point here, if it is any of your business."

"So, if you don't mind," Chloe repeated, "we would be very grateful if you could leave us to get on with our job. If your sister needs your help she will let you know."

Leon looked as though he was going to lash out at her, but then he clenched his jaw, turned round and left, banging the door behind him as hard as he could.

Chapter Twelve

Dear goddess, what an obnoxious specimen of manhood. Just seeing him around with Theano, I hadn't realized what he was like. And he obviously expects instant obedience from his sister – and every other woman who comes within his orbit, I shouldn't wonder. He really fancies himself. Imagine having to live with something like that. And he certainly didn't barge in here to help Theano.

I am not stupid, of course I know that there are different kinds of 'them', different sorts among those who have power and run things. But what a striking contrast, this arrogant patronizing strutting peacock, and Daphne's brother – and to him I was really rude and aggressive, there's no denying it.

Chapter Thirteen

Kleopatra's husband Phanes went to Daphne's prothesis with many misgivings. He wasn't fond of going to look at corpses anyway, and he couldn't see how he was going to be able to follow the instructions the priestesses had given him. He wasn't the right man for the job, but they didn't give him any choice. So here he was. Daphne looked beautiful even in death. 'What a waste', Phanes thought. Her mother Olympias was tearing her hair and crying. Her young brother Philippos was pale faced and silent, sitting on a stool by the couch, and her grandfather was crying noiselessly with ashes on his head. There were other people there as well. Phanes tried to blend into the background by babbling inanely for a few minutes – not that anyone seemed to pay any attention. He could see that slaves were coming and going, but there was no way he could just corner one of them and ask them questions. He shouldn't have come. It's as simple as that. He started moving towards the front door.

"I'll walk you out." Stephanos suddenly appeared at Phanes' side; when they had moved away from the others, he said, "What are you doing here? You didn't come to pay your respects to Daphne, you hardly knew her."

"I was sent as a representative of my mother-in-law and Chloe because they obviously couldn't come."

"So why are you looking so shifty? You've been looking guilty from the moment you came in. If I didn't know better, just from your face and shifty gestures I'd say you came here to steal.

But I know that's not true, I know why you are here; you came to snoop."

Phane was mortified. "It's not my fault. They sent me because they couldn't come. I didn't want to come."

"Is that so?"

"My mother-in-law and her colleagues are trying to find out stuff to show that Alexias is innocent."

"If he is innocent." Stephanos sounded forbidding.

"If he is. But they think he is." He hesitated and then went on, "Actually, I went to see him myself at the mayor's house, and he told me…" He stopped. 'Oh, gods, what am I doing?' Phanes thought to himself. 'They've addled my brains sending me here to do an impossible job, and when I am embarrassed I always babble. But I can't say that to him.' "Never mind, forget it. Sorry," he said to Stephanos.

"Oh, no." Stephanos sounded even more forbidding now. "You finish your sentence. You've insulted me enough by coming to this house to snoop, instead of coming to me to ask for the information you wanted. I am not going to put up with further insults. Now say what you were going to say."

"But you'll be more insulted if I tell you," Phanes whined. Stephanos said nothing. "All right, I'll tell you, but it's not my fault if you are offended. Alexias thinks that you killed Daphne yourself, and that when you prosecute him, you are going to bring false witnesses, to make sure the court find him guilty."

"The gods protect me from the half-witted! So he's another one who thinks I am the killer, is he?"

"Why, who else does?"

"The subpriestess, Chloe."

"No, no, I don't think so, I think she's keeping an open mind; she's looking at all possibilities."

"She is, is she? Never mind that, what do you want? Why

did you come here? What did you expect to find out?"

"They told me to ask the slaves some questions. Especially if there are any slaves Olympias brought with her from the city when she came to stay, who would know about Daphne."

"And how did you think you were going to manage that?"

"I don't know." He hesitated and then continued. "They told me I should try to catch one slave alone when no one was looking, and then offer him, or her, money to get him to talk to me and fix it for me to see the others as well."

"And did you do that?"

"You know I didn't, you've been watching me. I'm no good at this."

"Fine, then. I'll fix it for you. You have my permission to talk to the slaves. The ones Olympias brought with her are my slaves, and as for Philon's household slave, Philon is in no fit state to make any decisions at the moment, so I am giving you my permission to interrogate him as well. And you make sure you tell the priestesses that I did, do you hear? Now go in there," he gestured to a door that turned out to lead to a small room to the right of the entrance – Philon's house was very modest – "and I will send them to you." As he shut the door behind him, Stephanos smiled at Phanes' guilelessness. Of course he had not been insulted by the young man's attempt at snooping; it was almost comical – or it would have been, in other circumstances.

'How am I going to do this?' Phanes asked himself when he was left alone, waiting for the first slave to turn up. 'What am I supposed to ask? I can't do this.' But he could easily imagine what the priestesses would have to say about that, they would say "Don't be stupid, you know you've got to do it; just follow the instructions." 'Yes', he thought, 'I'll follow the instructions, and do my best; anyway', he cheered himself up; 'whatever I find out will be better than nothing, which is what they've got at the moment.'

In the end, he did find out something, in fact two things, as he eagerly reported to the three priestesses, after he had purified himself and returned to the sanctuary. He wasn't sure whether his first bit of information was relevant, but he gave it to them anyway, to show how hard he had been trying. It was about Daphne's younger brother, Philippos: he had refused to go to the Hunt with his mother and the others that morning, saying that he was feeling ill, but he had left the house immediately afterwards and hadn't come back until very much later, just before his mother's party had returned, before they knew about Daphne's death. He said he had felt better, and that he had gone to the beach and taken out his grandfather's little rowing boat.

Phanes' second piece of information was about Daphne herself, and he was convinced that it was very significant – though he wasn't sure what it meant, or what it had to do with the murder: one of the slaves Olympias had brought with her from the city had told Phanes that Daphne had visited, and presumably consulted, a Thessalian witch. And this had apparently happened in the city, over three months ago, just before Daphne had come to stay at her grandfather's house here at Philaidai for a short holiday. The slave had accompanied Daphne to the witch's house, but she had been ordered to stay outside, so she had no idea what Daphne had wanted from the witch.

Chloe was excited. "Now that is really important. We must find out more. If we find out why she went to the witch we'll probably find out more about her than we've ever known."

Someone had to go to the city to find the witch and ask her, but this turned out to be more of a problem than they had expected – or rather than Theano had expected. She'd thought that her brother Leon would do it for her; he loved riding and she thought he would be delighted to go, but when she sent him a message asking him to come to see her, explaining what she wanted, he didn't come; he sent a letter back saying he was too busy the next day. Phanes then offered to go if Leon would lend him a good horse. He didn't fancy riding to the city on one of the sanctuary's horses, he needed a good long-distance runner. But again, when Theano wrote and asked Leon he wrote back saying that he didn't have a good horse available just now, that one of his two good long-distance runners besides his own was lame and he'd lent the other one to a friend.

"Come on, can't you think of anyone who has good horses around here?" Chloe prodded Theano and Phanes.

"My brother-in-law." Theano suddenly exclaimed. "Nikias' brother, Leandros, he is bound to have a horsebreeding friend in the neighbourhood who may lend us a horse." And so it proved. The friend with whom Leandros and Hermione were staying to be near the sanctuary for the Hunt and the festival, who lived at Prasiai, offered to lend them a good horse, and so it was arranged that Phanes would pick it up and ride to Athens the next morning at first light.

After these arrangements had been made for the expedition to find the Thessalian witch in the city, Chloe turned to the other bit of information brought by Phanes, that Philippos had stayed behind during the Hunt, claiming that he was ill, but then had disappeared soon after the others had left.

"Do you think there is any significance in that?" Chloe asked Theano and Mego. "We are looking for unusual behaviour… But, of course, as we don't know anything about the boy we don't know whether this is unusual behaviour or not."

"Well, actually, there is something…" Mego remembered. "According to his aunt he's in love with one of the bears, though the aunt didn't know which one; that's why she thought he must be really ill if he didn't come to the Hunt where he would have been able to see her. But obviously he had other plans."

"If he was in love with one of the bears, he wouldn't have gone out on a boat when he could have been watching his beloved instead." Theano stated the obvious.

"Yes, it would make much more sense if he went to the Hunt alone, so that he could go looking for her in the woods, or meeting her or whatever, we don't know whether his love is requited or not. And Daphne may have seen him, and she may have threatened him with dire consequences..." Chloe didn't complete her speculation, but her meaning was obvious, even to Theano, who protested "Don't be ridiculous. Philippos adored Daphne. Anyway, he's only twelve years old."

"Your point being what? That people don't kill those they love, or that twelve year olds don't kill?"

"Neither, I mean both."

"And how would you know that?"

"What makes you think you know more than me? I've raised a son, and a daughter come to that, and you are not even married."

"Yes, well, whatever, just remember it's your son we are trying to save here."

"If Philippos didn't kill her he may have seen something," Mego mused.

"Surely, if he'd seen anything significant he would have said."

"He may not have realized it was significant, or he may have been in shock," Chloe speculated, "or he may have other reasons, depending on what or whom he saw."

"If anything; let's not get carried away, we don't even know that he was there, let alone that he saw anything."

"Still, we should talk to him as soon as possible."

"It's too late to arrange anything for tonight. We must wait until tomorrow, after the funeral."

As Chloe rose to go, Mego spoke hesitantly. "Maybe we shouldn't take anything for granted, you know. What we were saying just now, about Philippos maybe seeing something and not saying anything for some reason …it made me think. The bears were in the woods at the right time as well. Did anyone think of asking them whether they'd seen anything?"

After a short silence Chloe said, "I can't believe that they wouldn't have said if they had seen anything unusual, but you may well be right; maybe I didn't want to believe that they could have been so stupid, not to tell us if they saw something, even if it didn't seem important at the time. I ought to have thought of it myself, that we have to make sure, and actually ask them."

Mego tactfully moved the conversation on. "Do all the hunters stay together during the Hunt?"

"Not necessarily, it depends on how things go. I'll ask them what happened this time. I am going over to talk to them now. And if I find out one of them knew something and didn't tell…"

"What, what are you going to do about it?" Theano taunted her. "There's nothing you can do and you know it. They are graduating in a few days' time and that's that. They are out of your hands and out of your power."

"Maybe there is nothing you can do Theano, because power is the only thing you've got, but some people do relate to people in other ways…" Chloe paused and then went on, "Never mind that now… This is not the time. I'll go and talk to the group who went hunting with Kallisto. We know that the others just stayed in the clearing."

She went to the amphipoleion and took Kallisto and the other hunters out of their dormitory. She led them out to the inner courtyard, sat them down and asked her questions. The girls were indignant, especially Eunice. "What do you think we

102

are, morons, that we wouldn't have said if we'd seen anything out of the ordinary? Or anyone? You don't think we would have realized it was important?"

"Is that true of all of you? None of you saw anything?"

The other girls shrugged their shoulders. "Were you together all the time?"

"No, of course we weren't. We were supposed to be hunting, not strolling down the paths arm in arm," Eunice answered.

Chloe realized there was something wrong, something in addition to Daphne's death, that is, because she couldn't see how Eunice's aggression could have anything to do with Daphne. Eunice barely acknowledged Daphne's existence; she thought Daphne was 'even more stupid than the others.' And she wasn't normally gratuitously aggressive.

"What's going on?" she asked. "Why are you so angry?"

"I am angry because those two spawns of the Harpies, Zoe and Thekla, are making our life a misery more than ever, and we aren't supposed to do anything about it."

"What do you mean?"

Eunice recounted that morning's confrontation and explained that the two little girls were taking advantage of this policy and had gone on a rampage. She was supported in this by the other girls of her year group. Chloe then asked the younger girls who had been in the hunting party to go back to their dormitories and to send out the remaining girls of the older group. When the whole group had assembled Chloe started asking questions, beginning with the girls who hadn't been in the hunting party and hadn't heard Eunice's account. Their stories confirmed what Eunice had said, and Chloe was convinced. Then Eunice added that Zoe and Thekla had been unbearable ever since the arrival of the four adolescent helpers. "Right from

103

the start, they all took the view that the little ones are innocent angels, maybe a little bit mischievous, but basically, it's all our fault, and we shouldn't pick on girls younger and smaller than ourselves. In the meantime we are black and blue from all their pinching and tripping, as well as having our clothes messed up with dirt."

"Is that true?" Chloe asked the group.

The others said it was.

"Fine, I'll sort it out," Chloe assured them. 'Now go back to your dormitory. I'll sort it out, but not just now', she thought after they had left. 'I need some space tonight. It will have to wait until tomorrow, like everything else.'

Chapter Fourteen

The next morning the bears were to make their own way to the beach, while Chloe spoke to the helpers. She told them of the girls' complaints but she did not seem to be able to get through to them – maybe because she was feeling too exhausted to muster much energy. She was very fond of Anthea, Electra and Helena, but just now she could have throttled all three. Anthea was convinced she was always right, Electra followed Anthea's lead when it came to relationships, and matters of social intercourse in general, though she was much brighter and more talented than Anthea, and Helena just didn't care. They had made her angry, that combination of stubborn certainty on one side and indifference on the other, though she hadn't shown it. She wanted them out of her sight for a few minutes. She sent them ahead to the beach with Mego and told them that she would be joining them soon. She would go for a short walk by herself. It was very early in the morning and she thought she wouldn't meet anyone who would want to talk. But she met Stephanos. After Daphne's funeral was over, before daybreak, he had decided to go for a walk towards the beach. He told Chloe that he knew that she and the bears and the helpers would be there, Phanes had mentioned it, while he was babbling when he had first arrived at the prothesis, that Chloe was to take the bears swimming early in the morning.

Chloe couldn't tell, then or later, if it was because she felt emotionally exhausted and distanced from reality that she responded to this simple comment as she did, but she heard herself say, "And you couldn't resist the idea of so many naked little girls."

Stephanos' face jumped in surprise, then he laughed. "My inclinations do not lie in that direction, I can assure you."

"Oh, I see, you prefer little boys, then."

"No, certainly not. I don't find children sexually attractive. I cannot imagine how anyone can."

"Oh, really? And what is the difference between a ten year old girl and a twelve year old boy?"

"I have no idea, I don't fancy twelve year old boys myself."

"But you think it's a perfectly respectable age for a boy to be the beloved of an older man."

"People do, starting with twelve and upwards, yes, but if you are asking me personally, I haven't thought about it; it's not something that has ever concerned me."

"What do you mean?"

"Just that. I, personally, have never been attracted by boys or youths. Nor was I anyone's beloved. It's not compulsory, you know."

"Please, don't patronize me, of course I know. So what do you find attractive?"

"Fully grown women, what else?"

"Is that why you aren't married?" When she saw his surprise she added "We do have to know something about our girls' families, obviously. You didn't marry, so that you can indulge this attraction unhindered?"

"Many married men indulge this attraction unhindered, as you put it. But in fact, you are not as well informed as you think. I was married, but it didn't last long. I'm divorced now."

"I see."

"Right, then."

106

He made to go, but Chloe put her hand on his arm. "I'm sorry. I have obviously brought up unpleasant memories, and I embarrassed you as well, asking all these questions and saying the things I did. I don't know what came over me; light-headedness I suppose, from worry and lack of sleep. But before you go, I wanted to thank you for arranging Phanes' interrogation of your slaves yesterday."

"Did he find out anything useful?"

"Actually, he did. He found out that Daphne had gone to see a Thessalian witch about three months ago."

"Zeus give me strength!… I knew she was dumb, but…" he stopped himself, and then went on, "So what does this tell you? Apart from the obvious, concerning the efficacy of your teaching?"

Chloe decided to ignore his last comment. "We need to find out why she consulted the witch," she explained. "When we do, we'll know something important about Daphne that may be directly related to her death."

"Or not."

"Well, we'll soon know. Phanes has gone to the city to find the witch and ask her. Actually, he also discovered something else yesterday, and I wanted to ask for your help. Apparently your brother, Philippos, stayed behind when the others left for the Hunt, pretending he was ill, and then he went out immediately afterwards and didn't come back until very much later."

"Yes, my aunt was saying something about it, but I didn't take much notice. Philippos' doings are not exactly at the forefront of my mind just now."

"We think he may have gone into the woods on his own during the Hunt, and we wanted to ask him some questions."

"Why on earth should he want to do that?"

"It's complicated, but basically because your aunt thinks he's in love with one of the bears."

"But he's just a child."

"So are the bears."

He looked a bit bewildered, but then said "Well, I suppose, if that's what my aunt thinks, it's probably true. She's never wrong about this sort of thing."

"So could you arrange for me to ask Philippos some questions?"

"Yes, all right, I'll see what I can do. Obviously, you'll have to meet him outside the sanctuary somewhere, as he's still polluted, and you can't come to Philon's house. I'll try to organize something as soon as I get hold of him and I'll send you a message."

They said their goodbyes and Chloe walked to the little beach where the bears and the older girls were waiting and sulking.

"We've been here for ages doing nothing, waiting for you," Helena complained.

"Don't exaggerate." Chloe told her. "Is everyone here? Shall we start?"

"Actually Melissa isn't here yet," Kallisto said.

"Are you sure she hasn't already gone in the water on her own? It's not like her, to be late for swimming."

"Well, there weren't any clothes on the beach when Eunice and I arrived, and we were the first down," Kallisto answered.

"There she is," two of the youngest girls pointed to a figure swimming round the headland. As soon as Melissa came out of the sea, Anthea went up to her to scold her "What time do you call this? Are we supposed to wait here until you decide to put in an appearance? And why have you been swimming in your saffron robe?"

"There was no one here when I came," Melissa protested, "so I waited for a bit, and then I went for a walk, then I thought I'd swim for a bit, so I went to the next bay and swam over. I didn't want to have to do it both ways and wear myself out before we started our proper day's swimming. And I didn't take my clothes off because there was a man on the beach who was looking at me in a funny way."

"What man?" Electra asked.

But Anthea was not to be placated or sidetracked. "It doesn't make any difference if you are early or late. The point is we all had to wait for you."

"That's not true," Eunice objected. "We had to wait for Chloe anyway. We only waited a few extra minutes for Melissa. And you should be worrying about strange men watching us, instead of taking your foul mood out on us."

"That's quite enough," Chloe said firmly. "I am going to walk over to the next bay with Mego to make sure there are no strange men, and if there are, I'll take care of them. Now off you go, into the sea. You know the score; you are going to swim around the headland and into the next bay and back."

"Loyalties are interesting and strange things," she said to Mego when they were out of earshot. "They will stick up for their year group even when they don't like each other, like Eunice doesn't like Melissa."

"They are the oldest group, I take it."

"Yes, and at the moment they are having a running feud with the youngest group, or rather with two of its members, supported by the rest. And the helpers are not handling it very well. In fact they are making things worse."

"That sounds like fun."

"I could certainly have done without this, just at the moment."

"Oh, I don't know," Mego said, "maybe it's good to have something small to worry about; it takes your mind off the big stuff." 'I should know', she thought.

"Yes, well, maybe you are right. But this story about a man watching the girls could turn out to be both big and unpleasant."

The walk to the next bay was short, but by the time the two priestesses got there, there was no one on the beach. "Usually, we don't have to worry about things like that," Chloe said. "The local people look out for the girls, out of respect for the goddess and the sanctuary. And if they see anyone suspicious they don't know they deal with them. But the way things are at the moment…"

"Of course, the way things are at the moment, it could have been the girl's overheated imagination, and the man may have been a perfectly innocuous man walking on the beach."

"You are probably right. We are all so much on edge that we are probably seeing things. Still, it's better to be safe than sorry."

After the bears finished their swimming they had a short rest and then they practised some dancing on the sand. Then they sat around for a bit before starting back. Eventually they all returned to the sanctuary in a generally better mood, and they went on with all the things that had to be done before the beginning of the festival. At some point Chloe received a message from Stephanos saying that he hadn't been able to arrange her meeting with Philippos, because his brother hadn't been back to the house, in fact no one had seen him since the funeral. He would make arrangements as soon as he found him and would let her know.

Chapter Fifteen

Phanes had ridden out at first light. It took him about three hours to get to the city, and a bit longer to get back. He enjoyed the morning ride, in the fresh air, the sharp colours, the variety of intoxicating smells of multitudes of flowers, herbs and fruit that engulfed him as he rode past. But by the time he was riding back he was hot and tired and cursing his inability to say no to his mother-in-law – though, to be fair, he thought, this was truly an emergency and a matter of life and death. Mind you, whether what he had to tell the priestesses was worth the effort he didn't know. He had spent over two hours in the city; first looking for the witch – the slave's directions were rather muddled, he found, when he tried to follow them – then finding the witch, talking to her, and finally persuading her to tell the truth, which was the most difficult part, and he didn't know how he had pulled it off, more by luck than judgement, he thought, but he wasn't going to let them see that. He arrived back in the afternoon and reported in great detail. Despite everything, he felt proud of the way he had handled things. And why shouldn't he? He had got results, and that's what mattered.

He had found the witch, he told his mother-in-law, Chloe and Mego, and she had claimed that she didn't remember Daphne. Phanes didn't believe her, he was sure she would remember someone so beautiful, and young – he assumed most of her clients would be old hags, in which, as it happens, he was mistaken. But, as it turned out, he was right that the witch did remember Daphne; she was lying about it because she wanted to keep her clients' confidences, as her trade depended on her reputation for confidentiality. Phanes tried bribery, but that didn't work, and his attempt at threatening her only revealed that she had, or thought she had, powerful protectors.

"So I said to her 'All right, then, let her murderer go free, and Daphne unavenged, as long as you don't violate your lily-white professional code of ethics.' And then she said, 'What do you mean murderer and unavenged? Are you telling me she's dead?' And I said, 'Yes, of course I'm telling you she's dead. What do you think I'm doing here?' And then she complained that I hadn't told her this from the beginning, and I told her that I didn't think it was any of her business. She said that I was an arrogant pup, but then she asked me what we wanted to know. So I said we wanted to know why Daphne had gone to see her, and if it's true that it was over three months ago. And she admitted that she does remember her, not just because of her beauty, she'd gone recommended from a very good client, but she warned me that she wouldn't tell me who that was. Anyway, she told me that Daphne had gone to see her over three months ago, and that she had asked for a love potion for attracting a man who was taking no notice of her."

There was a short silence while the three women were digesting this information. Then Chloe jumped up and started walking about. "None of this fits Alexias," she said. "We now know that he had been in love with her for a long time, and she knew he did, and also the timing doesn't fit their having had sex just over a month ago."

"So there was someone else," concluded Theano. "Nikias was right. Alexias is a bloody fool, and that manipulative little tart… I could have killed her myself."

Chloe didn't remind Theano of her earlier protestations,

indeed fury, when Chloe had used those very words about Daphne at the Hunt. This wasn't the time. "There was clearly someone else. And this someone else is probably, certainly, I'd say, the man who made her pregnant," she asserted. "And he must live somewhere around here, since she went to see the witch just before she was coming to stay with her grandfather."

"Not necessarily," Theano objected. "It could have been someone who was visiting someone living around here."

"How would Daphne in the city know who was visiting whom around here?"

"She may have heard," Theano said. "Maybe her grandfather told her. Maybe that's why she was coming to stay with him."

"Maybe... But I can see from your reaction that the same thought has crossed your mind as well. Who is it who looks like a young maiden's dream, and who has refused to help us, and who showed unnatural interest in the murder, rather than in his nephew's imprisonment?"

Theano's face went red, and then she erupted. "You are being absurd. It's impossible. It cannot be Leon. He is madly in love with someone else, he's been wanting to marry her for almost a year, and he has high hopes, Agathe, the daughter of Agnon from Erchia, who plays very hard to get, Agnon I mean. Agathe's a virginal little thing, cocooned by her loving family, she couldn't be more different from Daphne."

"That gives Leon a very strong motive for killing Daphne, if she was pregnant with his child and she was threatening to make trouble."

"But why should he have slept with someone else, since he's so much in love with Agathe?"

"You aren't seriously asking me to explain to you why a man like Leon would have had sex with a beautiful girl who

113

threw herself at him, even though he was in love with someone else?"

"What do you mean 'a man like Leon'? And anyway, she wasn't making trouble; she was going after Alexias instead."

"Yes, but did Leon know that?"

"You don't have any evidence that it's Leon. It's just your spite and malice for my family. There are lots of men it could have been; lots of men live around here and they have lots of guests staying with them all the time."

"Maybe, but none of these lots of men came round to find out about the murder, wanting to know exactly when we think it happened, rather than show some concern about their own nephew being in custody. And he was stunned when we told him about Alexias having sex with her and being the father of her baby."

"But if he had been guilty he wouldn't have needed to ask about the time of death."

"He would, if he wanted to know what we knew, or thought we knew."

"But he wouldn't have asked in front of you two if he had anything to hide."

"Oh yes, he would, because he's arrogant, and he obviously thinks that women are stupid. Look, I am not saying I am right, it may not be him. But I am going to try to find out if he was Daphne's lover. Now that I know where to look, it shouldn't be difficult. There is always some disaffected slave or a neighbour, or someone who saw something."

"Leon isn't going to like it if he finds out you are asking questions about his private life," Theano said, rather hesitantly.

"I'm sure he won't, but he'll just have to lump it," Chloe replied.

Theano gave a funny laugh "You don't know my brother," she said.

"And what's that supposed to mean?"

"Nothing. Forget it." She hurriedly changed the subject before Chloe could press her to explain herself. "Let's pray that we'll find the murderer before the festival. Otherwise the goddess will be defiled, and we'll all pay the consequences."

Chapter Sixteen

Would the goddess really be defiled if a polluted murderer took part in the rites? Do we really know what the goddess wants? If death defiles her, why did she accept human sacrifice? Does Artemis really rejoice in human sacrifice? She didn't take Iphigeneia's life, she saved her, but the barbarians do sacrifice men to her – or so they say; of course, even if it's true, it could be that because they are barbarians, they think she wants human blood and they give it to her. On the other hand, she does accept it; and she did send fair winds to Iphigeneia's father after he had sacrificed her – or thought he had. But again, is it any worse that a virgin should be sacrificed to the gods than that young men die in battle? They say that's totally different. They say sacrifices have to be made to stand up for what's right. But don't both sides at war think they are standing up for what's right? – at least usually, not every single time, it's true, but in almost all wars; and they can't both be right. And if you look at the results, it doesn't look right at all, what we were told was the right thing to do. If the gods are happy with wars, what's so different about human sacrifice? And if the goddess accepts human sacrifice, does death really defile her?

Chapter Seventeen

The bears were reciting Homer. Chloe was listening at some level, while at the same time she was trying to work out a plan for finding out more about Leon. Had he really been Daphne's lover and the father of her child? She decided to let the girls have a short break. As she got up to go outside for a breath of fresh air Melissa rushed past her. 'Melissa', she thought. 'That's it.' "Melissa!" she shouted as the girl was running away. Melissa stopped; she came back, and stood waiting. "I assume your parents are still around. Are they still staying with that friend of your father's at Prasiai?"

Melissa looked puzzled. "Yes, they are, why?"

"Would you please go and make arrangements to send them a message saying that I want to see them here as soon as possible?" Now Melissa looked stricken. "What for? I haven't done anything. I swear. It wasn't me."

"It wasn't you who did what? Never mind, I'm not going to bother just now, whatever it is. Just go and do as I say, this has nothing to do with you, I want to talk to your parents about something."

"What?"

"Something that's none of your business. Now go off, and do as I asked you to."

After Melissa had gone Chloe wondered if she was doing the right thing, dragging a paralysed man out at a moment's notice. But she didn't have the time to go and see them at their host's house herself, and she really thought Melissa's parents were her best chance. They weren't Leon's kin, not really, while Alexias was Leandros' blood kin, so she didn't think they would be too reluctant to talk to her about Leon, and with Leandros' brother being married to Leon's sister, they were bound to know more about him than anyone else she knew except Theano, and she wouldn't talk. Or would she? If she realized that it was a matter of choosing between her son and her brother...

A couple of hours later Leandros and Hermione were shown into Chloe's sitting room, Leandros in a litter carried by two slaves, who left the room after they had deposited their master on a couch. Chloe was surprised to see that the faded blonde woman was very animated. In fact, she rushed to speak without waiting for the polite noises of greeting. "We came as soon as we received the message. What did you want to see us about? Is there something wrong with Melissa?"

"No, no, please don't worry. This has nothing to do with Melissa. I am very sorry if I worried you."

"What is it then? I can't imagine what you can want with us that doesn't concern Melissa."

"I want to ask for your help."

"Our help? What for? What help?" Leandros asked in an agitated voice.

"I need your help to show that your nephew Alexias did not kill Daphne."

"What? Don't be ridiculous, of course he killed her. What are you on about?" Leandros asked, in a puzzled voice.

"Have you seen your brother at all since the murder?"

Leandros looked somewhat shamefaced. "Not as such, I didn't think it was appropriate to butt in just now. But I did what I could to help; when Theano was looking for a horse for her son-in-law to ride to the city I found him one."

118

"Yes, I know. Well, that was part of the investigation into Daphne's murder."

"What investigation? I don't understand, what is going on?"

Chloe explained what had been happening and her thinking about the murder, 'our thinking' is how she put it, adding, "That's why it is important to find out if Leon was Daphne's lover, if he was the one who got her pregnant."

Leandros looked dubious. "I don't know if we can help you. We'll tell you everything we know, of course, but we don't know if he had sex with that girl. How could we?"

"Maybe you can start by telling me what you do know about Leon."

"Like what?"

"I don't know, start with his family."

"Well, as you know, it's a rich family, and very influential. Both parents are dead." He didn't seem to be able to think of anything else to say, so Hermione took up the story. "There were only the two children, Theano and him. He was born many years after her. Their mother had a couple of miscarriages and then two little boys, one after another, who died as babies. By the time Leon was born, and he lived to grow up, they would have given him the earth. That's why he was spoiled rotten and he turned out rotten."

"Steady on, old girl, that's a bit harsh."

"He's a rake," Hermione blurted out.

"Is he?" Chloe asked, looking at Leandros.

"He's a womanizer, certainly. Or so they say. I don't know about rake," he responded.

"Well, I do. He's a heartless rake," Hermione said firmly.

"That's just what you think, you don't know, you haven't got any evidence," her husband objected.

"Oh, yes, I do know. But you are right, I can't give you any evidence, because the last thing the poor girl I am thinking of and her poor mother need is for her reputation to be ruined. That's how he gets away with it."

"I see," Chloe said. "You are serious, aren't you? You do know something."

"Oh, yes, I do, I give you my word, I do. I'll swear an oath if you like."

"No, there is no need. I believe you. And thank you very much. You've given me what I needed. At least now I know he's the type to have sex with a young virgin, get her pregnant and then deny all responsibility."

"He's certainly that."

After the couple had left, Chloe went to see Mego in the guest suite and told her what she had found out. Then she summed up the situation as she saw it. "It does look as though it's Leon who got Daphne pregnant and then disclaimed all responsibility. He must have told her he wants nothing to do with her, otherwise she wouldn't have tried to foist the child on Alexias, sleeping with him and then telling him she's pregnant. And Theano is convinced that Leon wants to marry someone else, so he was bound to disclaim all responsibility for Daphne's baby. Or am I building too much on nothing? Maybe there was no other man, maybe Alexias is the father, and her visit to the witch doesn't mean what we thought it did. On the other hand, it was Bakchis who told me she was pregnant, and she thought she was much further along than just over a month. And it does seem to fit Leon's personality perfectly, that sort of behaviour."

"I think you are almost certainly right," Mego agreed.

"But where should we go from here?"

"It would be nice to have a more concrete piece of evidence."

"Yes, I know, but how can I get that? And if I did somehow

manage to get it, what should I do about it? Should I tell Stephanos? And at what point should I discuss the situation with Theano again?"

"Not yet, would be my instinct about Theano. Who knows, you may find that last piece of evidence falling into your lap."

"In my dreams."

"Perhaps. The gods may send you a dream that will make everything clear."

"In the meantime, I'd better go and get dressed for our dinner with the overseers of the sacred rites, or I'll be late and Theano will give me a public tongue-lashing."

Chapter Eighteen

Theano, Chloe and the four overseers of the sacred rites that remained in the sanctuary dined in the most formal of the dining room suites that were housed in the large building to the North of the temple. Its walls were decorated with a series of paintings on wooden plaques, representing several stories involving Artemis, and sometimes also her brother Apollo. It was an official banquet, so they were reclining on couches and they ate and drank off the sanctuary's golden plates and vessels. Not that the luxurious tableware and the fine food and wine made the diners any more cheerful. Chloe explained the situation 'as we saw it', stressing the importance of identifying the true murderer before the festival (which the overseers had worked out for themselves in any case), and setting out the various reasons why Alexias' guilt was very doubtful. The four men were disturbed by the possibility that a polluted murderer might participate in the rituals. After all, if things went wrong it was ultimately their responsibility. But they offered no practical help; they declared themselves happy to leave everything in the most capable hands of the priestesses, 'and the one of our number who is also the victim's legal guardian'. At least the discussion seemed to cheer up Theano, who began to contemplate the possibility that the destruction of her son was not a foregone conclusion.

After leaving Theano, Chloe was making her way to the amphipoleion; she felt soothed, and at the same time revived, by the smells of jasmine and honeysuckle and the familiar sound of the cicadas. The sky was ablaze with a bright orange moon and bright stars, and she felt a buzz at being here, walking in the sanctuary on a night such as this.

Suddenly, someone jumped out of a clump of rhododendrons and grabbed her from behind. She struggled to get away, but he was holding her in an iron grip. He turned her round, very roughly, and she saw that it was Leon.

"If you scream I'll kill you," he said.

Chloe decided (if decision is the right word for what went on) to bide her time and stay cool. "So you are saying you are a killer. That's interesting. What do you want from me?"

"My sister tells me that you think I was Daphne's lover and I killed her. And that you are going around asking questions about me."

"I haven't done very much asking yet, actually, I haven't had the time, but that's the idea, yes."

"I came to warn you, don't do it. If you do, if you disobey my orders, you'll regret it very bitterly. You'll find that I am a very dangerous man to cross."

Chloe smiled at him. "Thank you very much, I am really grateful," she said.

Leon's face turned dark red with rage. "What's that supposed to mean? Are you trying to make fun of me? I'm warning you…"

"No, not at all. I am expressing my sincere thanks because you gave me the concrete evidence I needed to confirm that you were Daphne's lover. I thought you were, but now I know. Your threats are confirmation enough."

"I don't care whether you believe it or not, but I didn't kill that stupid girl."

"Oh, really? You certainly had motive and opportunity. And obviously the right personality."

123

"I don't have to explain myself to you, but I am telling you, it wasn't me who killed her. Though now that she and her brat are dead I can get on with my plans without having to look over my shoulder. And I am certainly not going to let a jumped-up little daughter of a traitor wreck my plans."

"What difference does it make what I say, if, as you claim, you are innocent?"

"Your meddling can make waves, and things could come out that I don't want people to know about. Anyway, you are interfering with my business, and I won't have it. So I am giving you fair warning to stop."

"Or else?"

"You don't want to know."

"Oh, but I do. What are you threatening me with? Are you going to kill me too, as you said? Inside the sanctuary this time?"

"There's no need for that, there's more than one way to skin a cat. I know what's going to hurt you, and take the sting out of anything you say at the same time. I'll have you fired."

Chloe laughed. "You can't have me fired."

"Oh yes, I can. I can do that and even have you killed, if I can convince a court that you are practising witchcraft."

Chloe's laugh was more genuine this time. "Don't be ridiculous. Why should anyone believe you, or pursue such an absurd accusation?"

"Just because it hasn't happened before, it doesn't mean that it can't happen, it doesn't mean that a woman, even a priestess, can't ever be put to death for witchcraft; I'll prosecute you, and whip up hysteria, create a panic..."

"And how are you going to do that? Considering that I don't practise witchcraft, or indeed anything else that you could make appear to involve impiety?"

"You are so naive... I'll bring false witnesses; I am rich and

I am powerful; and who are you? The daughter of a traitor. Who do you think is going to bother to help you, if I decide to destroy you? You haven't got anyone. All you've got is a half-brother with little influence, even supposing he wanted to bother to use it on your behalf, which I doubt."

"There is the court, the jury…"

"Can you really be so simple, or are you putting it on? And you fancy yourself as clever. You think I can't manipulate public opinion, so that the jury think they know what's going on even before I bring on my witnesses?"

Chloe looked at him, bewildered. "And you would feel no scruple about doing it, would you? There really are people that have no principles whatsoever. You feel perfectly entitled to destroy anyone who annoys you."

"Why not? To protect me and mine, why shouldn't I? Help your friends and harm your enemies, that's the motto of all right thinking men."

"Like you are helping your nephew Alexias just now."

"Alexias is a hopeless case. You don't bother with hopeless cases. Anyway, in this case 'me and mine' is me."

"Of course it is."

"And I'm warning you. I will destroy you if you defy me. Don't forget, traitor's daughter."

"You obviously think you can use my father against me, but you are wrong. Whatever my father did or didn't do has nothing to do with me."

"That's not how the jury is going to see it. And they'll see the contrast. On one side a traitor's daughter, on the other me; my father died in battle, and my brother-in-law is a war hero."

"But you personally, you are not a hero, are you? It's just struck me, you know, what you remind me of. You speak like a woman. That's how women boast – my father died in battle, my

125

brother is a war hero."

Leon looked as though he was about to hit her. But, whether because he thought better of it, or because he heard a sound that turned out to be someone running towards them, he changed his mind. He gave Chloe a shove so that she fell down on the ground and then he disappeared.

The person running towards Chloe turned out to be Bakchis; she helped Chloe to her feet and told her "I was coming to find you. You'd better come quickly, we've got a riot on our hands." So Chloe, dazed and bruised, had to squeeze the turmoil out of her mind and focus on the disturbance. Apparently what had happened was that the youngest bears had sneaked into the oldest bears' dormitory to smear muck on their clothes. But the older girls had been lying in wait and ambushed them and wanted to punish them to teach them a lesson. The young ones went berserk and screamed the house down; they woke up the helpers, who rushed in to try to free and protect the small ones. And then all hell broke loose, because at that point the girls in the two middle groups, who had also been woken up by the screams, or so they claimed, and who had so far been neutral in the dispute between the youngest and the oldest, weighed in and stopped the helpers from rescuing the youngsters, who, they joined the older ones in claiming, richly deserved a beating.

Chloe knew that all this was an extreme version of what usually happened just before the festival, the girls' nerves being at a pitch before the big day, and also from the Hunt, only this time the murder and the rest had turned everything into hysteria. Still, a point had to be made. So she told the youngest girls that they were the ones at fault. That if they couldn't take punishment they shouldn't provoke it, and that what they were doing was fundamentally dishonest, attacking and provoking the older girls, and then playing the weak vulnerable victims to get protection from the helpers. And that she was was going to give them a punishment suitable to their persistent crime. She was going to tell them what that was going to be tomorrow. In the meantime they could stew.

"Yes," the older girls raised their fists in the air and jumped up and down.

Zoe and Thekla, the two ring-leaders of the youngest group, were indignant that they had been found out. "But how did they know we were coming?" they whinged.

"They knew because one of us overheard you and we told them," said one of the eight year olds, a pretty, graceful little girl called Pherenike.

"You see?" Chloe pointed out to the young ones. "You may take people in for a bit, and they play your game, but then they realize what's been going on and they turn against you. Let this be a lesson to you, together with the one you'll be getting tomorrow morning. Now you all go to bed, and I don't want to hear another sound out of any of you. Is that clear?"

They all nodded and then dispersed. But when the three helpers made the rounds of the bears' dormitories a few minutes later, to make sure that everyone had calmed down, Anthea discovered that Kallisto was not in her bed. She knew that it would be useless asking the other bears about it; she would have to try and find her. The little girl wasn't in any of the other dormitories, or in any of the empty guest-rooms, or in the courtyard or anywhere else within the amphipoleion – unless she was with Chloe and Mego who were closeted in Chloe's room and were not to be disturbed except in a dire emergency, which wasn't very likely. So Anthea went outside and started walking around the colonnade, very softly, so that if Kallisto was there she wouldn't hear her and run away. Eventually she saw a huddled shape on one of the benches that was almost hidden by potted plants. "And what do you think you are…" Kallisto looked up and Anthea saw she had been crying, was still crying, in fact, when she saw Anthea she burst into uncontrollable sobs. Anthea put her hand on the girl's shoulder. "What's the matter, why are you crying, has anything happened," she asked.

"Go away. Leave me alone," Kallisto said, in between sobs.

"I can't go away and leave you alone in this state. Anyway, you know you are supposed to be in your dormitory. I can't leave you out here."

"I don't care."

"Well, I do. Tell me what's happened, why you are so miserable."

"Nothing's happened, nothing new, it's just …it hits me from time to time."

"What hits you?"

"I can't tell you. We are not supposed to tell."

"What do you mean you are not supposed to tell? Is it something to do with the other bears?"

"What are you talking about? It's got nothing to do with the bears or anything else. It's private."

"Is someone in your family sick?"

"No. It's worse."

"Don't be stupid, Kallisto. There's nothing worse than illness."

"That's how much you know."

"If people are ill, they can die. Nothing is worse than that."

"My mother died two years ago."

"Yes, I know, I'm sorry."

"I still miss her, and I was devastated when she died; but at least the rest of us were okay, well, not exactly okay, everyone was devastated, but things were normal between us, they weren't all quarrelling with each other all time, like now that our family is ruined."

"What?" Anthea was stunned.

"Not totally ruined, but virtually ruined."

"Your family?"

"Yes, my family. Now you see?"

"But …how? What happened?"

"All I know is that it's my elder brother's fault, but I don't know anything else, or understand, and no one will tell me anything, except that according to my father we are not supposed to blame my brother because he meant well. Though it's all right for him, our father, to blame my brother and quarrel with him. And my other brother, Kallias, he said his life is finished. He was in love with a girl, and now he can't marry her. And he keeps quarrelling with father about that."

Anthea's interest suddenly moved up a gear. 'This may have something to do with Electra' she thought, 'or at the very least it concerns her, whether it's about her or not.'

"Oh?" She suddenly tried to sound casual. "Why's that, then?"

"I don't know. I told you, no one tells me anything. All I know is that it was complicated before, about this girl, but now he can't do it at all. It's a matter of honour; apparently, I overheard Kallias shouting that at my father."

"And why was he shouting at your father?"

"What is it to you? Why are you asking all these questions?"

"I was trying to help, understand the situation so I could help. But you don't want my help, fine. Now off you go, back in your dormitory. I'll be coming to check on you in a few minutes, and you'd better be in bed and asleep."

'Things are not as simple as they seem, then', Anthea thought. 'Is it possible that it's Electra that Kallias had wanted to marry? And that now they are financially destitute – or whatever – he can't, and that's why he cut her dead at the Hunt? And things were complicated before because she is an epikleros, and if he wanted to marry her the only way to make sure that a relative couldn't claim her and try to break up their marriage was to be adopted by her father. But in that case why has it become impossible to marry her now? Surely, his father will be much more amenable to the idea of his being adopted into another family now that they aren't rich any more?' She had to find out more. But she couldn't very well accost Kallias and ask, "Excuse me, are you in love with my friend Electra?" On the other hand, there are ways and means for other young men to find out at least some things that she couldn't. She decided to send a letter to her fiancé, Agias, summoning him to the sanctuary, and explaining roughly what she wanted him to do.

After she had dealt with the bears Chloe decided to talk things over with someone, ideally someone sensible, which in the circumstances inevitably meant Mego.

"How serious is the threat?" Mego asked, after Chloe told her what had happened.

"I don't know. I've never heard of a woman, let alone a priestess, been prosecuted for witchcraft, but that doesn't mean that it can't happen, he's right. It would be a charge of impiety or something like that, I suppose."

"And can he really corrupt the legal system, as he said?"

"Who knows? It's generally thought that juries can be easily manipulated, so, I suppose, they are not much of a safeguard; but I don't know."

"So what are you going to do?"

"What can I do? I have no choice but to carry on trying to find out what happened. I can't possibly let a murderer go free, let alone have him defile the festival, or any other rites, just to protect myself. I am a priestess, the city entrusted me with a responsibility; I can't just do what's convenient. Anyway, I don't want to."

"If he is the murderer."

"Why should he threaten me if he isn't?"

"It may be just as he said, because you would be making waves and this could interfere with his plans? He strikes me as arrogant enough to try to squash anyone who causes him even minor irritations."

"Whatever, I can't stop just to protect myself. At the very least he seduced Daphne and abandoned her and her baby."

"So what are you going to do?"

"I don't really know how I should set about things. Talk to Stephanos, I suppose. In the short term I need to talk to Philippos, if the blasted boy ever comes out of hiding. The first thing I've got to do tomorrow morning is find him and ask him what he saw at the Hunt."

"If anything."

"If anything."

Chapter Nineteen

Early the next morning Philippos was found dead in a small vineyard near the sanctuary, not far from the sea. The owner of the vineyard discovered the body almost as soon as he arrived to work on his vines, and he ran to the next vineyard and fetched the two brothers who owned it, and who were friends of his – not close ones, just the sort that are brought together by circumstances and topography. None of the farmers recognized the boy, but they had fought in the war and some things were clear to them.

"Look here. He was hit on the head, and he bled a lot. Of course, head wounds often do. This wasn't a natural death; he was murdered, just like that girl in the sacred wood."

"We should take him to the mayor's house."

"Yes, we'd better do that."

"This doesn't look like a fresh kill, does it?"

"No, you are right."

"When were you here last?"

"I wasn't here yesterday; I haven't been for a couple of days. Eh, you don't think they'll think I did it, do you?"

"Why should they think you killed a lad you don't even know?"

"Look at him, look at his age, look at his clothes. They could say I fancied him, that we all did, and as we knew we didn't stand a chance otherwise, with a rich and pretty boy like that, we forced him, and then we killed him so that he wouldn't't tell."

"Oh come on, they wouldn't say that, would they?"

"They might."

"You really think we are all in danger here?"

"Maybe. I don't know."

"Then we'd better take him somewhere else and dump him and let someone else find him. Or maybe you should. It's your vineyard; it's you they are going to suspect."

"I can't do that, that's real disrespect for the dead. The gods would make us all pay for that. And if anyone found out that we'd done it, they would be sure to think we killed him."

"So what do we do, then?"

"We should go and tell the mayor and have him come here and show him the body. There's nothing else we can do. Anyway, two bodies in three days, it's probably the same bloke that did it, and none of us was anywhere near the Hunt."

"You are right there. Let's go then."

So the two brothers went and fetched the mayor. He came with a couple of slaves who carried the body back to the village. Alexias was standing at the window of the room in which he was detained as they were going past; when he saw the dead boy he jumped on the windowsill and shouted at the mayor. "Is that Philippos? Is he dead? What's going on?"

"Do you know this lad?" the mayor asked.

"It's Philippos, Daphne's brother, Stephanos' brother; he's Philon's grandson."

The mayor really wanted to say 'Shit!', but he couldn't, so he instructed a slave to go and find and fetch Stephanos. When Stephanos eventually appeared he confirmed the identification. He seemed stunned.

Alexias, by contrast, was hopefully excited, for the first time since he had been found with Daphne's body. "You see, this proves I am innocent," he said to the mayor and Stephanos. "I couldn't have killed the boy; I was in here, with guards outside the window and the door. And this shows I didn't kill Daphne either. I told you I was innocent, and that's the proof."

"This is all very well," the mayor said, "but we don't actually know that the same person killed both the girl and her brother. There may be two different killers."

"Oh, come off it, how likely is that?" Alexias was scornful. "Two murders in two days, of a brother and a sister, and it wouldn't be the same killer?"

"You may have an accomplice," Stephanos said.

"Yes, I suppose that's a possibility," the mayor agreed. "I hadn't thought of that."

Now Alexias was angry; he turned to Stephanos. "It's you, isn't it, as I said all along. You killed them and now you are trying to blame me."

"I won't dignify that with an answer just now," Stephanos said, in a tightly controlled voice. "Just now I need to take my brother's body to be prepared for burial, and tell his mother and his grandfather and his aunt. So I am not going to deal with you just yet."

When Stephanos arrived at Philon's house with Philippos' body he sent a slave to fetch Olympias, Praxilla and Philon, with instructions not to tell them that Philippos was dead; he wanted to tell them himself. When he did, Praxilla threw herself against him, sobbing, and tearing at her hair, Philon collapsed and then rolled about on the ground, dirtying his hair, as he was supposed to, and wailing; Olympias shrieked an eerie shriek, and then it was like life was squashed out of her entirely. She went through the gestures of tearing her hair and messing up her clothes and all the rest, but it was like she was a moving toy.

Praxilla did her duty by Philippos' corpse, together with Olympias, she washed it, anointed it with perfume, clothed and adorned it with jewellery, and then laid it out on a couch for the prothesis. Then she purified herself to the extent that she could at this stage, which was not, of course, enough to allow her to enter the sanctuary, and she sent a message to Chloe, begging the subpriestess to come and meet her at her cousin's son's house at Steiria.

When Chloe heard that Philippos had been killed she immediately thought of Stephanos; she thought that this proved that her initial suspicions against Stephanos had to be right, for who else would want to kill a twelve year old boy but family? Then she remembered why she had wanted to see Philippos, that she thought he might have seen something when his sister was murdered, that he might have had information that could have led to the killer, and she felt better. In any case, she thought, Philippos' death exonerates Alexias. But then, she thought, not necessarily. He may have had an accomplice; not for Daphne's murder, but now, when his life was in danger, isn't it possible that his father might have killed a witness to save his only son, without whom his household would come to an end? That was a possibility that could not be easily discarded. Where was Nikias? She hadn't seen him since the morning of Alexias' arrest. She went to ask Theano.

"He's in the city," Theano said. "He left immediately after they took Alexias into custody at the mayor's house."

"That's very strange timing. Is he trying to distance himself from Alexias? Disown him?"

"No, not at all, how dare you say such a thing? He's gone to the city to engage an orator to write Alexias' defence speech."

"Already? But surely…"

"Actually, the real reason he's gone to the city is to rally support among his friends, you know, create the right climate."

"No, I don't know." After a short silence she went on.

"Presumably he would have done that even if Alexias had been guilty. In fact he probably does think Alexias is guilty, doesn't he?"

"I don't think this is any of your business, do you? I know you've tried to help Alexias, but that doesn't give you the right to interfere in things that don't concern you."

"Sorry. I only meant…" she hesitated.

"I know what you meant. And until you have a son whose life is in danger don't try to give me lessons in morality."

'It's no use', Chloe thought. 'She thinks I don't understand, and by her lights she's right. She thinks it's natural to do anything for yourself and yours, and she thinks everyone does it. Only an idiot would think otherwise, and she doesn't think I am an idiot, so I must be getting at her. Or I don't understand what it is to be a mother.' "Yes, fine," she said, "sorry" and she left.

"You see what I have to put up with?" Theano sighed to Mego, who had been visiting her when Chloe had come to ask about Nikias.

"At least she's doing all she can to help your son." Mego tried to be diplomatic, since it was Theano who was her ultimate hostess at the sanctuary; but then she thought 'What the hell, what do I care?' and continued, "If someone had been in a position to stop my son from being killed, I would have put up with anything from them for the rest of my life."

"You don't really think that I believe Chloe will save my son, do you? That I'm relying on her efforts?" Theano laughed. "Come on… I must admit I had got caught up in it for a bit, but then I realized, it's ridiculous, the idea that she would find the true killer and all that. Anyway, Alexias isn't really in danger, they'll let him go very soon. Nikias is taking care of things, you know, talking to people, and it's going to be all right."

"I see…"

"So there is no need for Chloe to agitate so much."

"And it doesn't worry you that the real killer may pollute the festival?"

"Oh, I'm sure the killer is far away by now, it was probably a stranger, as I thought all along. Why should he hang around to come to the festival?"

"Right, I see what you mean." Mego couldn't bring herself to pretend to agree, so she asked to see some more of the weaving patterns Theano had been showing her when Chloe had come to ask about Nikias.

Chloe had things to do, in fact she was very busy, but she also felt very unsettled, she had a lot of unresolved issues to deal with, so when she received Praxilla's message she made time to go and see her at her cousin's son's house. Alexandra, their host's wife, tried to stay around to find out what was going on, after all, her brother Andreas wanted to marry the mother of the two dead youngsters, but Praxilla told her very firmly that she needed to have a private discussion with Chloe. They went outside and sat in the garden, which reached down to the sea.

When Chloe offered her condolences, Praxilla thanked her and said that she wanted Chloe's help. "These two blows to our family, one after the other, and the second more disastrous than the first, we must have done something to offend the goddess. Please tell me what I should do to propitiate her."

"You know that only an oracle can tell you if you have offended a deity, and which one, and what to do about it. But you must not assume that you as a family must have done something to offend the goddess. Bad things happen. It's not always because people have offended the gods."

"Or it could be a curse, of course. Maybe Stephanos' mother had cursed Olympias when she was dying, maybe she cursed Olympias and any children she would have, and this is the result of the curse working its way."

"I suppose it's possible."

"Of course, you could say that Olympias offended the goddess when she destroyed my brother's marriage for her own gain …though you would expect Hera to be primarily offended by that; but maybe it is Hera who is sending the punishment. And then Daphne coming to serve Artemis as a virgin helper when she knew she was pregnant would have enraged the goddess, and so the goddess killed her."

"A human hand killed her; someone hit her on the head with a stone."

"Yes, but they were acting as the agent of the goddess."

"Maybe. And if you are right it's all over. Olympias has lost her children and she is left without issue and alone."

"And Daphne is dead."

"But Philippos didn't deserve to die."

"Who said anything about deserving?" Praxilla gave a bitter laugh. "The sins of the fathers, or, in this case, the mothers… You know how an ancestral curse can destroy a family. That's why we learn all the stories, Oidipous, and all the rest, so that we have some idea of how things work."

"Yes, but the curse works with the person's own personality flaws, they bring it upon themselves. Philippos was only guilty of childish mischief."

"Well, that's what put him at the wrong place at the wrong time."

Chloe looked speculatively at the elderly lady. "So you worked out that he may have seen something during the Hunt that was dangerous to the murderer, and that's why he was killed?"

"Why else? And I can't believe that he wasn't at the Hunt to spy on his beloved in private. Or maybe meet her, for all I know.

And then he gets killed. Of course, we have to assume that whatever it was he saw, he didn't understand its significance, otherwise he would have told someone."

"Unless he thought he should confront the murderer himself, and avenge his sister," Chloe said. "Maybe that's what he was doing when he was killed, and that's why no one saw him alive after Daphne's funeral."

Praxilla laughed. "I'm sorry to disappoint you, but I doubt that very much; it's much more likely that he'd gone chasing after the girl he was mooning over."

"But surely, he wouldn't have gone chasing after a girl the day after his sister was killed. I can't believe that, I thought he loved Daphne."

"Oh, he did. He adored her. But boys of that age, there is a callous streak, believe me. My guess would be that he thought he'd use his grief to get the girl's sympathy."

"I wish we knew which girl it is…" Chloe mused. "So… He went to meet her, or to wait to see her go by, we don't know which. Then what? Did he meet her? And then what happened? We have to ask the girls if they saw anything. Obviously, Philippos' beloved isn't going to say anything to get herself into trouble if she had been meeting him, but the others may know something, or they may have seen something. I certainly didn't, but then I had a lot of things on my mind, and I wasn't looking." She was silent for a few seconds, and then she went on, hesitantly. "What worries me is that there is one obvious person who had a motive for killing both Daphne and Philippos." She paused again. "Who would want to kill a twelve year old boy other than family?"

"You mean if our theory that he'd seen something at the Hunt is wrong?"

"Yes."

"Maybe a pervert?"

"If a pervert killed Philippos that wouldn't explain Daphne's murder, and the two have to be taken together. Let's face it, we don't actually know that Philippos had seen anything, in fact it's not very likely that he wouldn't have said something if he had."

"If he'd understood the significance of what he'd seen, yes. But he wasn't the brightest candle in the box, you know."

"Oh, no, I didn't know."

"Don't get me wrong, he wasn't stupid, it's just that both he and Daphne, well... I suppose I may be wrong; I was probably unfair, always comparing them to Stephanos in my own mind." After a short pause she went on. "What you are saying is that you think the killer may be Stephanos."

"I'm not saying it is, it's just that ...a child like Philippos, who else but family would have a motive to kill him? If our theory that he'd seen something is wrong, that is," she added quickly when she thought that Praxilla was about to protest.

"And what motive do you think Stephanos had to kill his brother and sister?"

"Half-brother and half-sister. Money. Doubling his inheritance."

"Why should he commit two murders to double his inheritance? He is a very very rich man."

"And he hated them."

"He didn't hate Philippos, and I don't suppose he quite hated Daphne either. Olympias yes, I believe he does hate her. But Daphne I think it's more that he resented her, and I suppose in a way he resented Philippos as well, but, believe me, the last thing Stephanos wanted was for his brother to die. He was glad he had a brother to continue their father's household, because it meant he didn't need to marry again and have children himself."

"How do you know that?"

"He told me."

"Why should he not want to get married and have children himself?"

"That's his business, but that's what he wants."

"But you can't be sure, can you, that he didn't kill Daphne and Philippos, for whatever reason?"

"Yes, I can be sure," Praxilla disagreed. "Do I get the impression that you want me to reassure you that you are wrong?"

"Obviously, I don't want their brother to be the killer, let alone when he's also one of the overseers of the sacred rites."

"I see." Praxilla smiled, and then shook Chloe's hand thanking her for her help.

Chloe went back to the sanctuary and interrogated the bears and the helpers one by one in the presence of Mego, but if anyone knew anything they weren't saying. None of the girls admitted to being the object of Philippos' devotion, and no one admitted to having seen anything or anyone strange – other than Melissa's 'strange man who was looking at her in a funny way'. That may or may not have been significant, but it was in any case a dead end. Since she hadn't seen the man before, he wasn't one of the known suspects for Daphne's murder, though if the murderer had been a stranger it could have been him – if Melissa was telling the truth, of course, if she wasn't trying to protect one of her relatives. If she was lying, that probably let out both Leon and Stephanos, as she wouldn't lie for either of them.

"I don't think she's lying," Mego said. "She mentioned the strange man long before any of us knew that who was where that morning was going to be important."

"I suppose you are right," Chloe replied. "Thanks for your help. I'll have to work out what to do as soon as I take the bears through another dancing session."

She went and joined the little girls, who were resting on the grass underneath the trees in front of the amphipoleion before their dancing session, just in time to hear Thekla issuing a challenge to the older bears for a competition of ugly faces; she said that she would provide a silver bracelet as a prize.

"As long as it's over by the time we are meant to begin the class," Chloe said, "you can do what you like. It's no skin off my nose if you crease your skins and get all wrinkled like prunes, pulling your faces about."

Kallisto wanted to take part in the grimace competition, but Eunice stopped her. "My mother told me never to pull ugly faces, whatever I do. As Chloe said, you get wrinkles; if you set your face in the wrong shape, twisted, it could stay forever like that, because the flesh will get loose and out of shape. My mother says people who make ugly faces get to look older and ugly. And I was never never to do it."

"Do you always do what your mother tells you?" Melissa jeered, suddenly at their side.

"Come on, don't try this with me," Eunice said scornfully. "It's not going to work. And to answer your question, no, I only do what my mother tells me when it makes sense. Otherwise I would be very stupid, doing things because my mother told me or doing the opposite of what she told me because people tell me I shouldn't do what my mother said."

"Of course, some people haven't got mothers to tell them things, and they've got to get them second-hand from their friends." Melissa laughed.

Eunice turned to Kallisto, who looked stricken. "Just ignore her."

Kallisto ground her teeth and smiled. "It's all right, don't worry. As if I would pay any attention to Melissa. And it's not as though my mother died yesterday. I've got used to it by now."

Eunice took Kallisto's arm and walked her away from the other girls, who soon became absorbed in the competition. Most participants screamed horribly while they were making faces, perhaps to colour the perception of their grimaces as more terrifying, or to inspire themselves to bend their flesh more energetically.

"Do you miss her?" Eunice asked Kallisto. "Your mother?"

"Of course I miss her…"

"Do you think about her a lot?"

"What's the point of thinking about her, and about her death? It's not going to bring her back."

"If you want to talk about it…"

"I told you, what's the point? It doesn't make it better, talking about it. It just makes me think about it, and I feel better when I don't."

"I can't imagine what it must have been like…"

"Then please don't try," Kallisto interrupted her. "Let's go back and join the others." So they did, in silence.

When the results of the competition were announced by Thekla there was some acrimony, but no tears; since the judges were Thekla and Zoe no one was surprised that the winner was one of their year group – though, to be fair, six year olds have more of an affinity with grimacing than nine – almost ten – year olds, so the judgment may have been just. But Chloe was amazed by the skill with which Zoe and Thekla had got the upper hand again after their earlier humiliation. Of course they could afford the prize, that was a consideration, but the idea was unbelievably sophisticated for kids their age. 'Or maybe it's just me who's always been retarded', Chloe thought.

Chapter Twenty

I don't suppose it's very likely that Stephanos killed his siblings to make himself even richer. Praxilla certainly doesn't think so, and she's known him since he was born. Unless she's trying to protect her brother's last surviving child, of course. But he would have to be insane. No, it wouldn't make any sense. I can't be sure that he is innocent, obviously, but… I don't know, maybe I can. Leon was always the most likely candidate. He has a solid motive for killing Daphne and he's got the right personality for it. And if Philippos had seen him where he wasn't supposed to be he would kill again without a second thought.

What should I do about Leon now? I can't go to Stephanos, not yet, at least, not in the circumstances. Should I discuss this with Theano? It is, after all, her son's life that's at stake here, as she keeps reminding me. But I know what she's going to say. She's not going to accept that her brother may be guilty. I can just hear her, turning on me instead. If I tell her about his threats I wouldn't be surprised if she ends up convincing herself that if Leon said it, it must be true, and that I am practising witchcraft on the side.

So, what should I do? I suppose one thing I can do, and kill two birds with one stone, is tell the truth about Leon to Agathe's parents; that will spoil his plans, and protect an innocent girl from a rake, almost certainly a murdering rake, and at the same time stir things up and wait to see what he does. I may even gain some allies with clout.

Chapter Twenty-One

Early the next morning Chloe made preparations to inform Agathe's parents of all that she had found out about Leon. She could not, of course, call on Agathe's father, Agnon, a man she didn't know, so she sent a message to Agathe's mother, Polyxena, saying she would call on her that afternoon to discuss something concerning Leon, who, Chloe understood, was one of their daughter Agathe's suitors. The morning passed slowly at one level, but as far as fitting in all the things the bears had to do – study and practise for the festival and everything that had to be done before the end of their service – it went all too quickly. Theano had gone to the city, to return at the head of the procession on the evening of the next day, carrying the ancient wooden statue of the goddess that Iphigeneia had brought to Brauron when she escaped from the barbarians.

The bears were fractious that morning, but no more than was usual in other years at this stage, Chloe thought. They had lunch by the sea, not on the sand, which felt like burning silver dust under their bare feet (they had taken off their sandals as a treat), but in the shade of a stand of pine trees. Eventually Chloe managed to disengage herself and leave for Erchia.

Agnon's house at Erchia was more luxurious than good taste and civic virtue would have dictated, but it was still within the bounds of (barely) acceptable ostentation. Chloe was expected and was immediately taken to the mistress of the house, Agathe's mother, Polyxena, who was sitting with Agathe in the shaded part of a colonnaded inner courtyard. A couple of slaves were sitting spinning a bit further along.

Polyxena was about forty, Chloe reckoned, though definitely mutton dressed as lamb, and she fancied herself. She was even flirting with the male slave who was offering her grapes in a bowl – or so it seemed to Chloe, but of course she wasn't exactly an expert in such things, she may have got it wrong. Polyxena had an angular face with a large mouth and an angular body, quite unlike her daughter, who was an angelic looking, curvaceous blonde, with a dim expression, or so Chloe thought. 'Just the sort to captivate an arrogant degenerate like Leon.' Pushing away these thoughts, she introduced herself, or started to, for Polyxena interrupted her. "Oh, we know who you are. You are the daughter of the traitor Aineias, aren't you?"

Chloe was stunned by the attack, for attack it obviously was. "My father was called Aineias, and he was found guilty of treason. Whether I believe he was a traitor or not is another matter, and it has nothing to do with what brings me here. I came in my capacity as subpriestess of Artemis Brauronia. I don't think that my late father's history can be of any concern to you."

"Oh, is that so?" Polyxena made her voice drip with disdain. "But our affairs concern you, it seems, a traitor's daughter who casts doubt on the verdicts of the courts."

"I don't understand why you are being so hostile. I came here to do you a favour."

"We don't need any favours from the likes of you, thank you very much."

"I came to do you a favour by giving you and your husband some information that I discovered about the man who wants to marry your daughter, to tell you what sort of person he is."

Polyxena's face was suffused with rage. "How dare you come here with your lies, and throw mud on a man who is so

146

high above you, you shouldn't be allowed to mention his name, let alone slander him in this shameless way."

"How do you know they are lies, since you haven't even heard what I was going to say? And if he's such a perfect gentleman with all the manly virtues, why hasn't your husband given his consent for him to marry your daughter, then?" She paused, but Polyxena said nothing; she had calmed herself down and was indicating disdain again, by picking grapes from a bunch, and eating them one by one, pretending to ignore Chloe, who went on. "You know, I risked a lot by coming here to tell you all this; your perfect gentleman Leon has threatened me with dire consequences if I don't drop the whole matter. I certainly didn't expect to get this sort of thanks from you."

"We didn't ask you to get mixed up in our affairs. And we certainly don't need your help," Polyxena said dismissively. "And anyway, you probably are a witch, what else would one expect from the daughter of a traitor?"

Through the blur of her anger, Chloe realized that Polyxena had revealed more than she could have meant to. She was clearly closer to Leon than Chloe had imagined. "Ah, so you know what he threatened me with, do you? That's very interesting. Well, whatever you think, I am going to tell you what I came to tell you, and you are going to hear it, whether you want to or not. At the very least your daughter deserves to know the truth. Leon deflowered a young virgin of good family, made her pregnant and abandoned her. He may even have killed her."

Chloe heard a gasp, coming, she thought, from the direction of Agathe, who until that moment had shown no reaction to the conversation, as though it had been conducted in a language she didn't understand; at the same time Polyxena jumped up and shouted "Get out of my house you despicable wretch, get out before I have you flogged."

Chloe had no choice but to retreat, if she didn't want to risk being manhandled by Agnon's slaves. As she was going she heard Polyxena reassure Agathe. "Don't worry, honey, we won't tell your father. Nothing and no one is going to stop our plans."

'Our plans?' Chloe wondered with the still functioning part of her brain, the part that wasn't drenched in misery, now that the anger was seeping away. As well as being utterly humiliated, she was stunned by the malevolence that had hit her, where she was expecting, if not gratitude, at least some kind of positive response. She wasn't going to give up trying to bring Leon to some sort of justice, make sure he got his just deserts, but she felt almost defeated, she really couldn't think what she could do next. 'The fact that Polyxena knew that Leon had threatened me with a prosecution for witchcraft suggests complicity', she thought. 'At least between her and Leon. I wonder what that means? And does she really believe that Leon was innocent? She must do, otherwise she wouldn't be so keen for him to marry her daughter, surely.'

She walked towards the crossroads where one of the sanctuary's carts would be waiting for her; she hadn't wanted to commandeer it, or indeed take a horse, just for this expedition, not with the festival coming up, and so much to be done, so she had arranged for the driver and two female slaves to pick up some supplies for the sanctuary from a farm just beyond Erchia. She was walking slowly down a road lined with rhododendrons, when she was grabbed roughly from behind. She was shaken, albeit barely surprised, when she saw that it was Leon. He must have been warned about her visit to Polyxena and he was now evidently waiting to extract whatever he thought he was entitled to extract from women who disobeyed him. Putting his face against hers he spoke in what Chloe thought could be best described as a hiss. (She was trying to focus on small things, and so drag her mind away from the menace that was engulfing her.) "I know what you've done. I warned you, and you didn't listen. You defied me, and now I am going to make you pay. Not that you managed to achieve anything, but you dared go against me."

Chloe knew that she mustn't show any fear. "So, what are you going to do, then? Kill me as well? You don't think another body might be a little difficult to explain?"

"If I wanted to kill you I'd kill you, and no one would know about it. No one knows I'm here." Leon's voice swaggered – if a voice can swagger, Chloe thought with the distanced part of her brain that was functioning almost normally. "Mego knows you threatened me; and Polyxena and Agathe, of course, but I know they are your puppets."

"A Spartan woman! Who is going to listen to a Spartan woman? Anyway, I said 'if' I wanted to kill you. I don't need to do that. I'll do it all legally, and make you really suffer. If it weren't for that I'd beat you black and blue, that would really give me pleasure, but it may complicate things when I prosecute you for witchcraft."

Chloe repeated to herself what she always said to the girls, 'You mustn't let a bully smell your fear.' "You are not still going on about that, are you?" she said.

"I'm not just going on about it, I've got everything arranged. I think ahead, you see, just in case you were too stupid to do as I told you. I've already prepared the ground, and I have found two excellent false witnesses. I'm going to teach you a lesson you'll never forget. Kiss your job goodbye, kiss your life goodbye, with any luck."

"That's up to the jury to decide; whatever you do, it's not up to you."

He laughed. "Oh, no, you can't be so naive, surely; you can't really believe that there could be a chance you won't be convicted and punished."

"Punished for what? I haven't done anything. You are the one who is guilty. You had sex with a respectable virgin, you then abandoned her, and for all I know you killed her."

"So what? Not that I killed her, but so what?"

"So you admit that you deflowered her and got her pregnant and then abandoned her. It's just the killing you won't admit to, but that's not surprising. Not that there was any doubt that you were the father of her baby, but it's interesting that you are prepared to admit it…"

"It's none of your fucking business, none of it. I told you before to butt out of my life. Now it's too late. No one goes against me, or tries to, and gets away with it."

"Is that so? How nice for you." She goaded him because her apparent calm seemed to enrage him, and that gave her some satisfaction, it stopped her from feeling she was about to be crushed.

"You fucking bitch!! I'm going to ruin you and I'm going to crush you to the ground. Going against me, and then having the cheek to talk back to me. Who do you think you are? You are a nobody."

"I am an Athenian citizen and the subpriestess of Artemis Brauronia."

Leon laughed, genuinely, or so it seemed to Chloe. "And you think that's going to save you? Do me a favour. You are the daughter of a traitor; you haven't got any kin with influence or power. I'm going to crush you and have you legally killed. Who do you think is going to stop me, eh? Who do you think is going to stand up for you, against me, you stupid woman?"

"How about me and my friends here?" Stephanos stepped out from behind a clump of rhododendrons, flanked by two men of about his age. "Do you think we might do as witnesses, telling what we just heard?" Stephanos asked a dumbstruck Leon. "You know my friends, Andron and Charias, don't you? Andron, you may remember, is one of the ten magistrates this year, he is the archon basileus. You can't have a more unimpeachable witness than that, can you Leon?"

Leon's face had turned green and rigid. "What are you doing here, how did you know…?"

"You are not the only one who thinks and plans ahead, Leon. I do. Agnon does too."

"Agnon?" Leon looked dazed "What has Agnon got to do with it?"

"Well, apparently Agnon didn't trust his wife as far as you were concerned, he had this feeling that she was trying to make their daughter fall in love with you, so she would pressurize her father to let her marry you. Agnon suspected that his wife fancied you herself and had sublimated it in this way."

Leon laughed.

"You can laugh as much as you like, but it's because of Agnon that we caught you out. He had bribed one of his wife's slaves to keep an eye on things, and especially on you, so when Polyxena received Chloe's message this morning and she summoned you and demanded to know what it was about, and you told her that you had had sex with Daphne, and you regretted it, that she had thrown herself at you, it was a moment of madness, and it meant nothing, but you hadn't killed her, and that Chloe was trying to frame you to protect the real murderer, and she said she would take care of Chloe, and you said that so would you, and explained how, the slave told Agnon, and Agnon came to me, because I was Daphne's guardian. So, I had you followed, and then I summoned my friends, who had been staying at Andron's summer house at Halai Araphenides, very handy for Erchia, and here they are. Here we all are, and we caught you red-handed."

Leon had recovered from his shock, and his confidence had been oozing back. "Doing what? You've got nothing on me."

"You obviously think you are dealing with idiots, and that you are going to bluff your way out of this, as you have done before, don't you? Well, I've got news for you; you aren't, not this time. This time you are not dealing with besotted or frightened women. I'll prosecute you as a sycophant for a start, we all heard you saying you were going to bring a malicious prosecution, and that's a very serious charge, as you know. Then, of course, we all heard you admitting that you deflowered my sister. If I had caught you having sex with her I would have been entitled to kill you on the spot. As it is, and now that she's dead, I am not sure how things stand, but I'll find out; we all heard you admit what you did. And then we'll decide about prosecuting you for the murder of my sister and my brother."

"But I didn't kill them. I'm not a murderer. None of that had anything to do with me. It's just that mad bitch who has it in for me."

"Well, we shall see, won't we?"

"Look, I really didn't kill your brother and sister and I can prove it." He paused, and then went on sounding more like his usual assertive self. "If I do prove to your satisfaction that I didn't kill your brother and sister, couldn't we come to some arrangement?"

"Some arrangement?"

"Yes, an arrangement between us. After all, we are all men of the world here. Your sister is dead, so the dishonour she brought on you is gone with her. And this malicious prosecution business, surely, there is malicious prosecution and malicious prosecution. I mean, this woman may not be a witch, all right, I admit that she isn't, and I made it up, but she is the daughter of a traitor. And I had my reasons for getting her out of my way. It's not as though I was going to accuse one of you, or your friends. I mean, she's not someone who matters, is she? And I can be a very useful ally, very useful indeed; and I will owe you."

Stephanos stared at him for what seemed like moments, but was, of course, only a few seconds. "It is true what they say. Some people can only see others through the filters of their own character." Turning to his friends he said, "I think he should be arrested for murder, don't you? We'll sort things out later."

Leon lost his cool again and grabbed Stephanos' arm, screaming, "No, no, I can prove I didn't do it. I swear I can prove it. I was somewhere else when Daphne was killed."

"So why did you never mention that before?" asked Chloe.

Leon looked at her contemptuously and ignored her question.

"Answer the priestess' question!" Stephanos ordered him, gripping Leon's upper arm. "And it's a very good question we would all like the answer to."

"Because if Agnon had found out I would never be able to marry Agathe. And he could have prosecuted me as well." Leon answered resentfully. "But now it looks as though I have no choice, thanks to you. I'll pay you back for all this, all of you, don't you worry. You'll see. No one messes with me."

"So…" Stephanos prompted him, "Are you going to tell us where you were when Daphne was killed or aren't you?"

"I was with Agnon's wife, Agathe's mother, Polyxena."

"What do you mean exactly, 'you were with'?" Stephanos asked, after a stunned silence.

"We had sex. She was supposed to be at the Hunt, but she came to my house instead."

"And she'll confirm that?" Stephanos asked in an exaggeratedly incredulous tone.

"I don't know. I hope so. She'd better. If she doesn't I'll bring proof that I know her body and I'll tell everyone."

"But you'll be confessing to adultery with a respectable married woman. The punishment for that is very severe," Andron said.

"It's not as bad as murder. And the jurors aren't likely to be a bunch of prigs like you, most men understand such things. And that's if Agnon does prosecute me, and he may not want to."

"Dream on," Andron laughed.

"But it doesn't sound possible to me," Stephanos objected. "How could Agnon's wife have managed to get away from where she was expected to be, to go and have sex with him? Especially since, we now know, one of her slaves was spying on her for her husband."

"I don't know and I don't care," Leon shouted. "I'm telling you the truth, that's what happened. She was crazy for me, and I wanted her on my side, to help me convince her husband to let me marry their daughter."

"What a gentleman." Chloe sighed.

"The subpriestess is right, you are a truly charming gentleman," Stephanos laughed. "Right, we'll check and we'll see. In the meantime we'll escort you to the house of the mayor of Philaidai, where you'll be kept under guard until we have completed our enquiries."

"I'll pay you back for this. See if I don't." Leon spat at the three men.

"You told us that already," Andron said.

"And you, you are going to pay worst of all," Leon said to Chloe. "It's all your fault, and I am going to get you. Look at you, a traitor's daughter, ugly and old…"

"But not, I believe," Chloe interrupted him, "quite as ugly or quite as old as the woman you just told us you bedded to get to her daughter."

Stephanos, Andron and Charias laughed. "She's got you there." Stephanos taunted Leon.

'They are feeling sorry for me', Chloe thought. 'Never mind', she told herself. 'The important thing is that I won and Leon lost, and I am safe.'

Chapter Twenty-Two

Stephanos, Andron and Charias, with Leon in tow, escorted Chloe to the crossroads, where the sanctuary cart had been waiting all this time. Stephanos then suggested that he and Chloe walk back to the sanctuary – in his case to the gatehouse of the sanctuary, since he was still polluted from the death of Philippos, whom he had buried that morning before dawn – accompanied by one of the slaves, for propriety's sake. They had things to discuss. She agreed.

Andron and Charias left with Leon and Stephanos, Chloe and the slave started walking slowly towards the sanctuary. At Chloe's suggestion they went through a pine grove, which provided a short cut. Stephanos said, "I can't believe this man. No conscience, no notion of honour, nothing. No ethical dimension whatsoever. Just me...me... He obviously doesn't think he did anything wrong, to Daphne, or to you, and he feels very aggrieved that he didn't get his way."

"I know. He thinks he's entitled."

"That's it. He does believe he's entitled, you are right. I've come across people like that before."

"And I believe that it's exactly that sort of person who does kill; they see no reason not to, if someone is in their way."

"You may be right. He's certainly a much more plausible candidate than Alexias – if his story about sleeping with the mother of the girl he wants to marry doesn't check out, or if he still had time to kill Daphne anyway, whether or not he had sex with Polyxena."

"That was a pretty revolting revelation. Or am I too much of a prude?"

"No, you are right; it was a pretty revolting revelation. Sleeping with the mother in order to ensnare the daughter... And it wouldn't have stopped there, either, is my guess. If he did marry the daughter, he would have gone on sleeping with the mother as well."

"But he loved Agathe. That's the one thing that rang true in the whole story."

"I am not doubting that he loved her. But do you think that would have stopped him having sex with her mother? Not someone like Leon. Especially if Polyxena pressurized him, if she told him that she would tell her husband and daughter he'd had sex with her unless the relationship went on."

"Do you think she would do that?"

"Why not? She was having sex with him when he was trying to get engaged to her daughter."

"Why do you think she did it?"

"I don't know. Maybe she likes sex and Agnon isn't any good at it. Maybe she likes variety. Or maybe it made her feel young, sleeping with a younger man who wanted to marry her daughter."

"That's disgusting."

"No more disgusting than when dirty old men do it."

"Oh, I agree absolutely. But it's still disgusting."

They came out of the pine grove and walked in silence under the olive trees that were lining the road.

"What about Alexias?" Chloe asked eventually. "What are you going to do about him?"

"I won't be prosecuting him. It's obvious that the two murders are connected and he couldn't have killed Philippos. We don't know how they are connected, but whatever the case may be, the only person who might conceivably have been prepared to kill to save him, his father Nikias, was in the city throughout the time when Philippos could have been killed. We checked that. So Alexias has to be innocent." Chloe thought that Stephanos' chain of reasoning was not totally watertight, but her instinct was that he was right, Alexias hadn't killed Daphne. "So he'll be set free," Stephanos continued. "The mayor and I agreed that we'll let him stew for another night and then let him go tomorrow morning. His troubles won't be over, of course; he'll have to face his commander when he rejoins his unit at Rhamnous, and his punishment for leaving his post and coming down here is not going to be lenient, I can tell you."

They walked in silence for a minute or so. As they were approaching the village Chloe felt the smell of jasmine and of honeysuckle beginning to seep into the air as the light was darkening. Then she asked, "So, if it isn't Leon and it isn't Alexias, who do you think did it?"

"The short answer is, I don't know. But I have been wondering about someone else, Andreas, you know, the man who is in love with Olympias, his sister is married to a kinsman of my aunt Praxilla's – and of mine, I suppose, come to think of it. He has been hanging around obsessively ever since Daphne died. He's always hung around our house, but now he's just totally obsessive, he follows Olympias everywhere he's allowed to."

"He may be trying to give her moral support, of course. To gain credit, and make himself indispensable, so that she'll come to rely on him and agree to marry him."

"I suppose it's possible."

"On the other hand, you may be right. You remember when I had that conversation with Alexias, just after Daphne's body was found?"

"How could I forget?"

"Well, he was calling Andreas an old pervert, and he told me that Daphne was dead against him marrying her mother, and that she had told her mother that Andreas had made sexual advances to her. Her mother didn't believe her, she got very angry and told Andreas, and he was apparently rude to Daphne, and threatened her – though it's not clear what with, a good smacking would be my guess, and that's if that part of the story is true. I certainly didn't take the rest seriously, though if it had been true that would give Andreas a good motive. However, knowing Daphne, I'm afraid I don't believe a word of it, and Mego and Theano agree with me. She obviously made it up to turn Olympias against him, but it didn't work, because when it came to manipulation Daphne was still an apprentice to her mother. But of course Andreas may have felt threatened, he may have been afraid that if she were prepared to go to such lengths, she might eventually manage to convince her mother not to marry him. And now you say that he's become even more obsessive about Olympias… Did he have the opportunity to kill Daphne and Philippos?"

"Probably. Definitely Philippos, I should say; he came to the house after Daphne's funeral, but Olympias went to her quarters, and so he couldn't stay for very long. As for Daphne, probably, I think. I asked, and no one could swear that he was there with the others at the Hunt all the time, except his sister, but she would say anything to protect him."

"So you think that he may have killed Daphne because he was afraid she would convince her mother not to marry him. And Philippos? Had Philippos seen something he didn't realize was important?"

"Maybe. Or maybe Andreas thought that Olympias wouldn't marry him because of her children, and that with her son dead she wouldn't want to return to her father's house, so maybe she would marry him."

"Is she likely to do that?"

"I don't know, perhaps. But she seems utterly devastated. I don't know if she would want to start a new life. She is… different, it's difficult to explain, it's as though she's sunk into total despair."

"But that doesn't mean that she will stay like that forever; after all, it's very early days yet. She will probably pull herself out of it eventually, and start living some sort of life again, even if she is unhappy. And even if you are right, and she has gone into permanent decline, Andreas couldn't have known beforehand that this was going to happen."

Stephanos thought for a bit and then said, "You know, you may be right about her starting to think about some sort of future for herself. Something happened this morning I was going to tell you about, and now you made me think again about Olympias' behaviour, which I thought was a bit bizarre, even for the circumstances."

"What happened?"

"I'll tell you, but let me ask you a question first, out of curiosity, but it's connected with what I've got to tell you; weren't you surprised that I was so easily prepared to believe the story when Agnon sent me a message, and act on it, that I didn't stop to check?"

"I was assuming that you trusted me, the information had come from me."

"Ultimately it did. But in fact, what happened is that by the time Agnon's message reached me I had already discovered that Leon had been Daphne's lover, and that he was responsible for her pregnancy."

"How?"

160

"Let me tell you the whole story. Yesterday, after Olympias and my aunt had laid out Philippos' body and my aunt left to meet you..."

"You know about that?" Chloe interrupted.

"Yes, of course I know about that," he answered somewhat impatiently. "Who do you think encouraged Praxilla to come to you, personally?"

"Oh."

"Anyway, after Praxilla had left, Olympias, who until that point seemed to be half dead herself, erupted into the room I have been using as an office in Philon's house and started screaming at me and accusing me of having killed Daphne and Philippos. She was yelling that it could only have been me, because who else would have a motive for killing a twelve year old boy." Chloe blushed with embarrassment, as she thought that Praxilla may have told him that she herself had said the same thing. "I tried to argue with her," Stephanos went on, "to explain that I had nothing to gain and quite a bit to lose from Philippos' death, but she went on screaming and trying to attack me. It was not just distressing, but also very embarrassing, as people were going to start coming for Philippos' prothesis at any moment, and they would have heard her hysterics, the house is rather small. Anyway, her father heard her, and he came in and eventually calmed her down and then he told her that I had no motive whatsoever for killing Daphne and Philippos, unless I was insane, and if I was she would have seen some sign of it before now, as we've been living in the same house for all these years; and he also told her what Praxilla had told him, that Philippos may have seen something when Daphne was killed, and not realized its significance. Or he may have gone after the killer himself, to avenge his sister. She liked that idea. He also said something else, which I found very touching in the

161

circumstances. He said that if she's so stupid that she can't recognize a good man when she sees him and lives in his house, he hadn't managed to teach her anything at all, not even the little he had thought he had. Anyway, she left, and later on she sent me a note asking for my forgiveness. And then this morning, after Philippos' funeral was over, and we went back to the house, she came to see me." He paused. "It was extremely disturbing. She fell on her knees on the floor and grabbed my knees, and begged me as a suppliant to find the killer and punish him." He stopped.

"What did you do?"

"I tried to raise her, of course, and make her sit down, but she wouldn't, until she'd said what she wanted to say."

"But why did she feel she had to beg you on her knees as a suppliant?"

"That's what I said; I told her that of course I was doing my best to find the killer and prosecute him, and she said that she had no one else to ask, she was alone and the only person she could turn to was me, her enemy, and she knew I didn't care for her children, but she begged me in the name of Zeus the protector of suppliants. So I told her again, that of course I was going to try to find their killer, that they were my siblings, and that even if they'd been strangers I'd like to think I would have done something to help them get justice. And this went on for some time." He paused. "And what you said just now made me suddenly think that maybe this wasn't just about me finding and prosecuting Daphne's and Philippos' killer. Maybe she was also asking me to accept her, not to throw her out of my house. Now that her son is dead, she has no claim on my father's household and on me, other than the return of her dowry, of course, and she thought I was going to throw her out, in which case she would have to come and live with Philon, a long way from the city, and

162

without …well, you know, the standards of living she's become accustomed to. Call me cynical, but now I thought of it, I really believe, without doubting her pain and her desire to get vengeance for her children, I believe she was killing two birds with one stone, finding a way in, after yesterday's scene; that's why she was begging me to do my duty, as though I wouldn't have done anyway."

"I'm sure you are right. But she probably also assumed you would behave as she would if she were in your position."

"I suppose... Anyway, when she took it in that I was already trying to find the killer and punish him, I asked her what she knew about the deaths, or anything else before that could be relevant that I didn't know about. And she told me about Leon. She said that Daphne had told her that she had been in love with him, and slept with him, and then she got pregnant and when she told him he threw her out of his house and said he would deny everything and bring his friends as witnesses that she slept around with different men."

"Poor Daphne!"

"Up to a point poor Daphne. Because she also told her mother that she knew Alexias had been in love with her for ages, so she was going to seduce him and then convince him the child was his and make him marry her."

"And her mother didn't try to stop her?"

Stephanos laughed. "What do you think? This is Olympias we are talking about. She had probably taught Daphne these things in the first place."

"Poor Daphne!"

"I suppose, but ultimately we must all take responsibility for our own actions, After all, who made Olympias what she is? How far back do you want to go?"

"But Daphne was so young."

163

"Not so young that she didn't know she was destroying Alexias' life."

"I agree, but he did have sex with her."

"Can you imagine a callow youth like him saying no to the stunningly beautiful girl he has adored from afar for a long time? Being a woman, I know that you may not quite understand, but believe me, he couldn't."

"Are you saying that no man can resist a beautiful woman throwing themselves at them, whatever the circumstances?"

"Not at all. I am saying that this particular callow youth couldn't resist the stunningly beautiful girl he's adored from afar for a long time."

"Anyway, she ended up by destroying her own life. If the two are connected, her deceiving Alexias and her death... Is that all Olympias told you? Didn't she know anything else?"

"No. Except that she knew, or thought she knew, she wasn't sure, that the girl Philippos was besotted with was Alexias' cousin Melissa." He paused and turned to Chloe, smiling, "So you see why I was ready to believe Agnon's story about Leon straight away. For this at least we should be grateful to Olympias, that I didn't waste any time trying to check it."

Chloe thought Stephanos looked exhausted. "It can't have been easy for you, dealing with Olympias in this state, either today or yesterday," she said, after a short while.

"It was horrible. I wish I didn't have to deal with her at all, I wish I didn't have to see her ever again. I have hated her for so long, and now she's totally shattered and I can't even feel happy about it." He walked in silence for a while, and then went on "She did ruin my mother's life, you know – and mine. She set out to seduce my father, and she succeeded; he divorced my mother and married her. And my mother... I know she just willed herself to die in the end."

"How old were you at the time?"

"It started before I began my ephebic service. He divorced my mother and married Olympias while I was away."

"I am so sorry."

"Yes, well …there you are…"

He looked very sad. Chloe tried to distract him, or at least to pull him back to the present. "So what are you going to do about Olympias now?" she asked. "Are you going to let her stay in your house?"

"I don't know. The last thing I want is to have her living in my house, as you can imagine. On the other hand I can't bring myself to throw her out, if she wants to stay. It would be cruel, and though she deserves it, I couldn't bring myself to do it, when she's lost both her children."

"You wouldn't be throwing her out on the streets. She would be returning to her father's house, which is what is supposed to happen when widows have no sons."

"I know but …her life has just been shattered, and having to leave the city as well… And her father is not wealthy, and she's become used to luxury."

"You'll be returning her dowry, so at least she'll have that."

Stephanos suddenly brightened up. "That's an idea. When I return her dowry, I could give her an extra dowry, I'm sure there wouldn't be any legal objection to my doing that, whether or not she wants to get married again, I'll look into it." He was becoming more animated. "Or I could find someone, some kinsman or other, living in the city who would be prepared to have her stay in his house if I pay him enough. The best thing for everyone of course would be for her to agree to marry Andreas – if he's not the murderer, that is."

Chloe liked walking and talking with Stephanos. From time to time she allowed herself the fantasy that any moment now he would turn and touch her. But each time she quickly called herself back to reality. Eventually, she asked, "Were you the only child of your father's first marriage?"

"No, just the only one who survived; I had a younger brother who died as a toddler and an older sister who died when she was ten. She was called Praxilla after our aunt." He looked far into the distance, hesitated, and then went on. "She was a truly special person, my sister. I knew it even then, though I was very young, and after she died everyone spoke of her when I was little, of how exceptional she was, how kind and how bright, and how ...I don't know, special, gifted." He stopped again, hesitated again, and then continued. "I suppose that was one extra reason why I resented Daphne. Instead of having my own special sister, I lost her, I lost my mother, and in return I got that ...that...self-obsessed imbecile. I know she wasn't born until many years later, and she wasn't responsible for my sister's death, but she was for my mother's, at least her mother was, and Daphne..." He laughed a sad laughter. "Can you believe our father preferred Daphne to my sister Praxilla? I could see it every time I saw the two of them together, Daphne and my father. I suppose being a rather simple man he felt more comfortable with a beautiful girl child who could wind him round her little finger with pouts, compliments and whatever other wiles women like Olympias teach their daughters..."

He looked grimly ahead and quickened his step. Chloe desperately tried to find something to say, to break the silence, but her mind had gone blank, and she couldn't think of anything, except something that she knew she shouldn't talk about, but before she could stop she heard herself say, "Your aunt told me that you were happy that you had a brother, because Philippos could continue your father's household, so you didn't feel the obligation to get married again and have children."

166

"I know she told you."

"Where you so badly hurt in your marriage?" Chloe asked.

Stephanos said nothing.

Chloe felt mortified. "I'm sorry. I shouldn't have asked you that. I'm really sorry, it was crass of me."

Again, he said nothing for some seconds and then he replied. "No, I wasn't badly hurt. It was my fault. It was me who divorced her."

"Oh, I see."

"No, I don't think you do." Stephanos sounded angry. "I had no reason to divorce her, she was a good wife, and I wasn't after some other woman."

Chloe wasn't sure whether she was supposed to say anything, ask anything or what; she knew she had stepped over the line.

"Well, aren't you going to ask me what happened, then?" He still sounded angry. Chloe tried to apologize again, but he went on, as though she hadn't spoken, still in the same angry voice. "I wouldn't know what to tell you if you asked me. I don't know how to explain it. And you aren't going to think very well of me if I try. I was bored. There didn't seem to be any point – other than what they tell us is so important, having children, sons to continue our household. I just didn't see any point to the marriage."

He stopped. Chloe risked a question. "Did you love your wife when you got married?"

"Whatever love may be... I assumed one was supposed to get married, and I was madly attracted to her, which I now realize was lust, but had then thought that it was what people meant by love, and I was happy. But then ...gradually day in day out... Anyway, one day I decided that was it, and I thought it was kinder to divorce her quickly, before we had any children, so that she could make a better match afterwards."

"That was very generous of you." Chloe wasn't sure whether she was being ironic or not, but Stephanos answered her as though she were not. "Not really. I didn't care very much about having children; I didn't care at all, in fact. By that time Philippos had been born, so I knew there was someone to continue our father's household; and if I ever decided that I wanted a son myself I could always adopt one. There didn't seem to me to be any point being married to a woman I felt nothing for other than mild affection."

"These are very unusual views for an Athenian man to have."

"I am a very unusual Athenian man," he said, smiling. "I thought you'd noticed."

Chloe wanted to give a witty reply, but she couldn't think of anything to say.

"Of course, so are you," Stephanos went on.

"A very unusual Athenian man?" Chloe made the obvious reply, obvious and stupid she thought after she had said it.

But Stephanos laughed. "Woman, priestess, person, whatever…"

Chloe was relieved to see that they were approaching the sanctuary. She would have liked the walk to have lasted a lot longer, but she felt that she had made a fool of herself at the end, asking all those personal questions, and then not being able to think of something interesting and witty to say. 'Oh, well', she thought, 'so what? I'm not going to see him again, except in public, with a lot of other people.'

Chapter Twenty-Three

When Chloe returned to the sanctuary she went looking for Mego, to bring her up to date with the developments, but also just to talk to her. She felt like she was bursting with the need to tell someone what had happened, but she couldn't find Mego anywhere. Anthea said she thought that the Spartan priestess may have gone for a walk, and could she and Helena come and see Chloe, please? There was something they needed to talk to her about, very urgently.

Both girls looked very solemn as they came into Chloe's sitting room and sat down. Anthea gave Chloe a piece of papyrus which was inscribed with what at first glance looked like a letter. "Helena found this in her chest this evening," she said. "Read it." Chloe read it, and, eventually, and with some difficulty, because her brain felt sluggish, having been overstretched (she thought) by the events of the day, managed to make sense of it.

"This seems to be a letter addressed to Electra's father. It is accusing Electra of having loose morals, of sneaking out of the sanctuary during her stay as a helper to meet various young men." She looked at the two girls.

"It's all complete and utter lies," Anthea asserted. "Electra has never met a young man on her own in her whole life. And anyway, she's is in love with Kallisto's brother Kallias, and she thought he was interested, but then he cut her dead at the Hunt."

"Are you sure she hasn't been seeing other young men?"

"I am totally certain. It would be funny, if it weren't so

serious for poor Electra; she's tongue-tied at the mere idea of talking to a young man."

"I absolutely agree," contributed Helena. "This is sheer and total malice."

"But who wrote it? And why did they put it in Helena's chest?" Chloe felt drained by the day's emotional turbulence, and she found it more and more difficult to focus on this new problem.

"You can see it hasn't been sent," Anthea said. "Don't you recognize the handwriting?"

"Yes, it does look vaguely familiar, but I can't pin down whose it is."

"I recognized it immediately the moment I found it," Helena said. "It's Daphne's handwriting."

"You know, I believe you are right. Let me check." Chloe rummaged in her desk and found a list of timetabled activities for the bears which she knew had been written by Daphne at her request. She compared the two and confirmed that Helena was right. It was indeed Daphne's handwriting.

"But what does this mean?" Chloe puzzled aloud. "Why did Daphne write an anonymous letter to Electra's father?"

"That's easy." Anthea interrupted. "Out of malice and malevolence; to make life difficult for Electra, turn her father against her, make sure he refuses to adopt anyone Electra wants to marry. You notice it advises him to marry her off quickly to a mature and wise man. That's to make sure poor Electra doesn't stand a chance. Because making people unhappy gave Daphne a buzz, especially poor Electra."

"I am sure you are exaggerating," Chloe demurred.

"No, she's not exaggerating," Helena asserted. "Daphne did get a buzz when she made other people unhappy. And she took against Electra from the start – well, I don't know if 'took against' is the right way of putting it; more like Electra became her designated victim."

"Actually," Anthea said, "I think I can guess what triggered this off. I bet she wrote the letter the evening before she died. What Electra said to Daphne, that her own brother can't stand her."

"What you told Electra to say to Daphne," Helena interrupted her.

"Whatever. That would have rankled with Daphne. It was humiliating, especially with everyone there, including a foreign visitor, and that's the one thing she couldn't stand, Daphne, being humiliated, loosing face. So she was going to take her revenge on poor Electra."

"In other words, it's your fault, for telling Electra how to get at Daphne," Helena accused her, "it proved a bit too effective."

"Don't be ridiculous, it's not my fault. It's Daphne's fault. She was a nasty piece of work, even worse than I thought, and I'm surprised no one had killed her before now, if she went about like that."

"That still doesn't explain where the letter comes from, or why it surfaced just now," Chloe remarked.

"Maybe someone took it from Daphne's chest after she was dead and now they want people to know about it."

"No, we searched her chest immediately after she died when we came back to the sanctuary," Chloe told them.

"Maybe not soon enough," Anthea speculated. "Maybe someone got there before you; after all, you didn't come back to the sanctuary for ages. Or someone may have paid a slave to search her belongings. Probably the killer."

"But why was the letter put in Helena's chest now?"

"To make mischief. To make it look like Electra had a motive for killing Daphne."

"But she could only have had a motive if she'd known about the letter. And she can't have done," Chloe objected, "How could she? Anyway, she couldn't have killed Daphne; the three of you were together all the time at the Hunt."

The two girls looked at each other and then Helena said "Ah, well, not quite every minute…"

"But that doesn't mean that Electra was on her own for very long, none of us were. It's just that we weren't all three together every single moment, and it's not easy to remember now for how long each of us was on our own. But I can tell you that there isn't the slightest chance that Electra could have killed Daphne," Anthea asserted forcefully. "No, this is someone making mischief."

"But who? And why just now? Who had access to your chest, Helena?"

"Anyone living in the amphipoleion, and anyone who could bribe a slave. I mean, who can blame them if they take bribes to do something as innocuous as that?"

"Well, we'll interrogate the slaves tomorrow. Let's hope we'll get our answer then. Or at least part of the answer." Chloe rose to indicate that it was time for the two girls to leave. As they were leaving, Anthea asked, "How is Alexias? Are they going to let him go now that Philippos was killed while he was under guard at the mayor's house?"

Chloe decided to be discreet; after all; Stephanos had confided in her, he didn't intend to tell the whole East coast. "I don't know," she answered. "Why are you asking?"

"No reason, I just wondered. Melissa asked me if I knew what was going on. He's her cousin, you know."

"Yes, I do know. And listen, not a word about the letter to Electra. There's no point in upsetting her, she's obviously the one person who knows nothing about this letter, and we'd better keep

172

it that way until we know what is going on."

After Anthea and Helena left, Bakchis came to discuss some arrangements for the next day. With Theano gone Chloe was now in charge of the sanctuary – officially, as well as in reality – and it was just as well with all these crises that she had organized everything well ahead of time, and run through the tasks with every single person involved in the conduct of the festival. After Bakchis left a messenger brought Chloe a letter from Stephanos. This is what it said.

To the subpriestess Chloe, daughter of Aineias, from Stephanos, son of Satyros from Melite, greetings.

After taking my leave of you I visited the mayor of Philaidai and we decided to ride to the house of Agnon at Erchia to interrogate his wife Polyxena before the news of Leon's detention had reached her. She denied that she had visited Leon on the morning of the Hunt, and that she had ever had sex with him. She professed herself to be horrified by the idea, and she threatened us with dire consequences for besmirching the reputation of a respectable Athenian citizen wife. As she had eluded the surveillance of the slave paid by Agnon to spy on her – a fact the said slave had not reported to Agnon until now – it was her word against Leon's; and, of course, both had a lot to gain by lying.

However, Agathe had been listening at the door, and she suddenly burst into the room, followed by her father, who had been watching her spying on our conversation with her mother, and she, Agathe, told us that she had seen her mother sneaking away while they were on their way to the Hunt, and she had followed her. She saw her going to Leon's house, which was deserted – she had assumed that all the slaves had gone to the

173

Hunt, and that her mother was visiting Leon in secret.

So now Agnon is, of course, divorcing Polyxena because of her adultery. But when Polyxena realized that there was no point in lying any more, she told us enough to make it clear that it is extremely unlikely that Leon could have had the time to kill Daphne.

After sending the letter to Chloe, Stephanos returned to Philon's house. From tomorrow he would be able to go back to the sanctuary, after a final purification. He went to see his aunt Praxilla, who was in her bedchamber, and he told her everything that had happened that day.

"I can't say that I am surprised to hear that Leon is such an evil creep," Praxilla said when he had finished. "I have always found him singularly unpleasant, even as a small child. Poor silly Daphne…! And that poor woman, Chloe, to be threatened and humiliated for trying to do the right thing."

"You should have seen the way she stood up to him, though she knew that her whole life was at stake. She was magnificent. And when he tried to insult her, calling her ugly and old, she made him look an utter fool."

"What an unpleasant piece of work!" Praxilla sighed, and then added, "I wouldn't have said Chloe is ugly and old, myself. Would you?"

"No, no, of course she's not. She's a very attractive woman. But degenerates like Leon only lust after unripe flesh."

"Still, it must have been an extremely unpleasant experience for her."

"It certainly was, but I'm telling you, she handled it magnificently. Some would say that she handled it like a man, except that after seeing Leon's behaviour today I have to say that Chloe is worth ten men like him."

Praxilla smiled. "You see, I've always told you that not all women are either silly and vapid, or vicious and manipulative."

"Yes, well, never mind that. The thing is, what I wanted to ask you is, am I doing the right thing, letting Alexias go?"

"How sure are you that he didn't do it?"

"As sure as I can be in the circumstances. He certainly didn't kill Philippos, and even with Daphne, as Chloe pointed out, there were too many difficulties, things that don't fit the theory that he killed her. On the other hand, none of those amounted to conclusive proof that he didn't do it, and it's not impossible that someone else may have killed Philippos on his behalf. It's not very likely, and I don't think that's what happened …but it's not impossible."

"And…?"

"Well, who else is there? I know I didn't do it. It now looks as though Leon couldn't have done it, so who else is left?"

"It could be anyone."

"Yes, but why should anyone else want to kill Daphne? Her life was circumscribed, family, sanctuary in the last few weeks, and, as we now know, lovers…"

"There may have been other things about her that we don't know. We didn't know about the lovers, after all."

"True, but her mother did. And she would have told me if there had been anything else."

"Yes, that's true," Praxilla agreed. "At this stage she would have told you anything she knew."

"Well, it may have been a stranger after all. Maybe we have to rethink the whole thing, think seriously about the possibility that it was a stranger."

"But you told us she hadn't been molested, sexually. Was that a lie, to make us feel better?"

"No, no, she hadn't been sexually attacked, but a stranger

may have killed for another reason."

"Like what?"

"I suppose she may have seen something she wasn't supposed to see, something criminal, or whatever; no one was expecting anyone to be at the place where she was meeting Alexias at that time."

"And they would kill her for that?"

"It would depend on what she saw. If it was adultery, it would depend. If it was, say, incest, I should think they would kill her without a second thought, but again, it's difficult to guess how people like that think."

"What do you mean people like that?"

"People who commit incest – or even adultery, actually."

"Oh, don't be such a prude, Stephanos. All sorts of people commit adultery, but they wouldn't dream of killing anyone."

"It depends on how much they had to lose. Or it could have been something entirely different. Not of course murder or robbery, since there was no other victim, but it could have been something even more sinister, like conspiracy and even treason."

"But it would have to have been people she knew and recognized, or at least knew and recognized one of them; otherwise she wouldn't have been any threat."

"Yes, sure, so it could be one of the people we considered who had the opportunity, only for a motive we don't know. For example, Nikias had the opportunity; we just didn't think that he had a serious motive, not at that particular moment in time. Nikias is a calculating man; he wouldn't have taken a rash action over Alexias at that stage. But if Daphne had seen him doing something he wasn't supposed to…"

"Nikias couldn't have killed Philippos, though."

"As far as we know he couldn't have done, but we haven't checked as thoroughly as that, not to be a hundred per cent certain. Maybe we should have done. And anyway, if it is a conspiracy, his co-conspirator could have done it, or co-conspirators, if there are more than one."

Praxilla hesitated and then said, "If we are looking for odd behaviour in people Daphne knew, I think I should tell you that my friend Kallisto's family were acting very strangely when I joined them after the Hunt was over."

"And you think it may have had something to do with Daphne's death?"

"No, not really, it's just that, as I said, if you are looking for odd behaviour in people known to Daphne, I thought you should keep it in mind. Having said that, Kallisto was upset, but I can guarantee that she didn't know anything about a killing or anything like that, nor did Kallias, because he went berserk when he heard that one of the helpers had been killed, and then he calmed down when he found out it was Daphne. But Kallimachos and his elder son, I don't know. They weren't very sociable towards me, but I thought it was because they were generally in low spirits, only now I wonder. I mean, if they had been responsible for Daphne's death they would have felt strange having me around..." she paused and thought. "But that wouldn't work, would it? Because Kallisto and Kallias were also upset, and as I said, they certainly didn't know anything about Daphne's killing."

Stephanos got up. "My mind's gone stale. I think it's time to go to sleep." He kissed Praxilla's cheek. "But the way things stand, I think I'll have no choice but to have Alexias released first thing tomorrow morning. And if I am wrong, and he is the killer, or one of the killers, I'll just have to hope he won't flee the country."

Chapter Twenty-Four

When Chloe read Stephanos' letter she went looking for Mego again, and this time she found her. She told Mego everything that had happened since that morning. Mego commiserated over the humiliation Chloe had suffered at the hands of Polyxena and the terror at the hands of Leon.

"Still, she's clearly had her comeuppance and so has he. All is well that ends well," she added.

"But that's it, that's the problem, it hasn't ended," Chloe protested. "We still don't know who the killer is."

"I know, but at least your own problems have ended, and Leon's threats have turned against him, and he's going to pay for it, thanks to the intervention of the handsome Stephanos." Mego said with a smile, which Chloe ignored.

"But," she rushed to change the subject, "as I said, we still have a serious problem. If Leon isn't the killer all our main suspects are now eliminated."

"Could it have been a stranger after all?" Mego asked hesitantly.

"I really can't see it. She wasn't raped, and what could she possibly have seen, what could possibly have happened, to make her murder the lesser of two evils? If they were strangers who did whatever they did, what harm could she have done them, since she wouldn't have known them?"

"Unless they hadn't been strangers in the sense of people that Daphne didn't know, just in the sense that they didn't seem to have any connection to her."

"I suppose it's possible," Chloe admitted. Then she went on. "Let's try to think this through systematically. I'll go with my instincts and say that it wasn't a stranger in any sense. And it wasn't Stephanos. We have to look for a credible motive and at the same time a personality like Leon's, someone who feels entitled to everything they want."

"All right, then, what about motive? Who benefitted from the murders?"

"I thought Stephanos did, but it really is absurd that a man as rich as that should kill his siblings to get even richer. I don't know, maybe what I mean is that it's absurd that this particular very rich man would kill his siblings to get even richer."

"I can accept that. Who else?"

"Nikias and Theano benefitted from Daphne's death, because Alexias won't be marrying her; and they benefitted from Philippos' death because Alexias will be set free as a result. But Nikias couldn't have killed Philippos, and neither could Theano, she was in her house surrounded by sanctuary slaves coming and going, admittedly not as early as daybreak, and Philippos may have been killed as early as that, immediately after the funeral; but Theano surely wouldn't have been able to get in and out of her bedroom and her house and out of the sanctuary unseen, could she? Anyway, what am I talking about, she couldn't have killed Daphne, that's a physical impossibility, apart from the fact she hadn't known about Alexias and the pregnancy then."

"Maybe she had."

"I suppose she might have done, but she still couldn't have killed Daphne, she was involved with the ritual and under the eyes of very many people, including you and me, all the time."

"What if Nikias killed Daphne and Theano killed Philippos?"

179

"No, it doesn't fit. Killing Daphne at that stage would have been too extreme for Nikias; and killing Philippos to give an alibi to Alexias is too cold-blooded for Theano, even if she had managed to get in and out without anyone seeing her. And she's not really a great actress to carry it off like that."

"What about Kleopatra and Phanes?"

Chloe laughed. "No, that I cannot take seriously; even if they wanted to, if they felt that strongly about Alexias, which I haven't seen any signs of, they wouldn't have been able to carry it off, and they haven't got the personality for it."

"So?"

"So, we are back where we started. More or less." She paused, and then slapped her hand on her forehead. "Oh, no..." she said, "I can't believe I could have forgotten. There is something else. Mind you, I think it's a red herring as far as the killer is concerned, that's probably why I forgot, though so much else has happened today that it's no wonder..." Chloe blushed, as though she had thought of something that embarrassed her. She told Mego about the malicious anonymous letter that Daphne had written to Electra's father, which had suddenly appeared in Helena's chest.

"She really was a nasty piece of work, Daphne," Mego remarked. "I take it from what you've said that you don't consider Electra a serious suspect."

"No, she's not the type. And the girls tell me the accusations of immorality against her were all lies anyway. Which is what I would have guessed myself."

"I am not so sure you can say who is and who isn't the type to kill."

"I disagree, I think you can. Or rather, I think you can say that some people would not commit murder, whatever the pressure, and that some others would definitely do it in the right circumstances; with a lot of people I would agree that you can't tell. But I believe that with some you can, and Electra is one of them."

"My second point was going to be that, of course, whether the accusations were true or not, Electra would have suffered if her father had received the letter and believed it."

"Yes, but she wouldn't kill for it. If she found out what Daphne was doing she would tell Anthea or me and ask us what to do about it. That's how she came to annoy Daphne so much in the first place. She took Anthea's advice about what to say to Daphne, and she was all too successful. In any case, Electra didn't have the opportunity to do the murders, not really. Not without a lot of luck and incredible time juggling and the ability to become virtually invisible."

"But if she really did have lovers, as the letter claimed, then one of them could have killed Daphne, or Philippos, or both, to protect her."

"No, that's one point about which Anthea, Helena and I are totally certain about. She didn't have any lovers. I swear to you. I know. There is no way."

"I am surprised that you think one can be so certain about people's personalities. Everyone wears a mask and acts a role in my experience."

"You may be right in general, and I do know that I am a rather naive sort of person. But I think that there are certain types of people that you can tell what they are like. Especially when they are so young."

"But a skilful deceiver will be able to pretend they are precisely that type of person," Mego objected.

"Yes, but she had no reason to mount this elaborate deception all these years that I have known her."

"Maybe she wanted to be liked."

Chloe shrugged her shoulders. "All I can say is that this is what my instincts are telling me, honed by a long experience of young girls. I know you have an even longer experience yourself, but I know these particular young girls. Electra would not kill, and certainly not over something like that. Daphne now, nothing would surprise me." She paused, and then went on. "You know, I was wrong earlier, when I said that the letter isn't relevant to the murder. It is relevant, not because of poor Electra, but because it shows how far Daphne was prepared to go. Yes, of course; we all knew what she was like, but we didn't know the unbelievable extent of her malevolence. Given that, there may have been a whole set of people we don't know about who had a motive to kill her." She started to walk around in Mego's room. "So we now have yet another potential motive for her murder. If we try to go through things systematically, I would say we have one, two, three, four, five categories of motives: one, all the different motives relating to her affair with Leon and her pregnancy; two, the motives relating to her attempt to get Alexias to marry her; three, the motives relating to her family; four, any motives that may be relating to her having seen someone she knew do something they shouldn't at the Hunt; and now, five, we also have her malevolent activities.

"You don't think that the fact that someone is telling us about these malevolent activities just now may suggest that her malevolence and its consequences are not the real motive, and they are trying to divert our attention?"

"No, I think you are giving this person too much credit. I think someone is trying to draw attention specifically to Electra. Why, I don't know, but I am sure it was directed against Electra."

"But why just now? It's as though the killer knows that we are running out of suspects, and he's giving us a new one to divert our attention."

"I don't agree. Even if he knows about Leon, this thing about the letter must have been arranged before Leon had threatened me, let alone before it all came out about him and his alibi. So that doesn't work. In fact, we can't even be totally certain that it was the killer who left the letter in Helena's chest – or arranged for it to be left."

"Why should someone else have done it? It must be the killer trying to divert attention from himself – or herself."

"I don't know why, I'm just saying that we shouldn't discard the possibility that it wasn't the killer without further thought. For example, it could be someone continuing Daphne's campaign of harassment against Electra out of loyalty to Daphne."

"I didn't think Daphne was popular, who would feel that sort of loyalty to her?"

"Melissa, for one. She had a crush on Daphne. Or maybe Thekla and Zoe had taken the letter, and now brought it out to make mischief."

"Maybe, but I don't think so. I think it was the killer."

"It probably was, but anyway, we'll see what we come up with when we interrogate the slaves tomorrow. Moving away from the issue of motive for a moment, I still can't see how the killer knew where to find Daphne, if the murder was premeditated. Unless we can work out the answer to that we have to assume that it was an opportunistic murder, and I don't believe that, it doesn't make sense."

"Unless the killer was indeed Alexias after all."

"Let's sleep on it. Maybe the answer will come to us in our sleep. Maybe the goddess will tell us in a dream."

Chapter Twenty-Five

My thoughts are bubbling, and I can't sleep; but I have to sleep, tomorrow is a very big day for me, and the day after an even bigger one. I must try to shut the turmoil out. I will think about soothing things, good things. But what good and soothing things are there to think about? Thinking about Leon's humiliation isn't going to help. I can't just think about the good ending without thinking about the bad part before that. And it was really bad. I've got to shut it out of my mind; it makes the blood bubble inside my legs. There is nothing I can think about that doesn't stir me up. Maybe I'll think of nice places, being in nice places, on the beach, a sandy, silver soothing beach, walking with Stephanos... No, there is no point in fantasizing. I shouldn't let myself do it. Or should I? Why not? If I do, it makes me feel all warm and nice inside. If fantasizing about him can make me feel good, then in a way, at some level, it's a real experience, so why not? It's not as though I am likely to start imagining that it could come true – and that's where the hurt and the dangers lie. And I'm not going to show him how I feel obviously. I am not a silly adolescent.

Chloe woke up in terror and jumped out of bed. The nagging horror that had been just below her thoughts last night before she'd gone to sleep had burst into the surface while she was asleep. There was only one possible explanation. It all fitted, and it was the only thing that fitted everything. She tried to think things through systematically in her own mind before she told anyone else or did anything about it. Leaving aside motive for the moment, since that was the part she wasn't certain about – not that she didn't know what it was, she was sure she did, but she had no proof – everything else fell into place.

'Oh, Lord Zeus!' She suddenly thought, 'I must stop them from releasing Alexias. I must write a letter to Stephanos and send it off immediately, middle of the night or not, or else I might be too late. He must arrange a meeting at the mayor's house as early as possible tomorrow morning.'

Chapter Twenty-Six

Anthea woke up before dawn and sneaked out of the helpers'
dormitory and out of the amphipoleion to meet her fiancé Agias,
who was waiting for her at a prearranged spot under a palm tree.
After they had kissed and caressed each other – within definite
limits set by Anthea, who, she told herself, was not a fool like
Daphne – Anthea asked Agias for a report. He knew she wasn't
going to be happy about what he had to say.

"I'm sorry to disappoint you, but I couldn't find out as much
as you wanted me to. I don't know Kallias very well. I couldn't
very well suddenly turn up and ask him what's wrong with his
love life, and is it Electra he's in love with, and if it is why is it
impossible for him to marry her?"

"So what did you find out, if anything?"

"Don't be like that. I did my best. And I did find out
something. And you owe me big big time."

"Go on, then, what did you find out?"

"This girl he's in love with, when he wanted to marry her
his father wouldn't let him, but now his father is virtually forcing
him to marry her, but he can't do it, because it would be
dishonourable. I'll tell you exactly what happened, and then
you'll see what I put myself through for you. I turned up at their
house and said I was at a loose end and had come to see Kallias.
He wasn't very welcoming, but when he realized that I was
determined to hang around, and I wasn't going to go away,
unless he actually asked me to leave outright (and that was very

embarrassing I can tell you, I can't believe I let you make me do this), anyway, he suggested we went for a ride. They are all in a foul mood in that house; I can see why having a stranger turn up uninvited wouldn't exactly thrill them, especially since Kallias and I were never friends, just acquaintances. So we went for a ride, and when we stopped to rest our horses and we sat around for a bit he asked me whether I thought honour was important; I said yes, of course it was, and then he asked me if I thought it was more important than happiness, and duty to family. I did my best to avoid giving him a straight answer, to get him to open up. Anyway, bit by bit, that's what I put together in the end, what I told you. That when he wanted to marry this girl he's in love with his father wouldn't let him, but now his father wants him to marry her, but Kallias thinks it would be dishonourable."

"But that's brilliant. That gives us the answer."

"How do you work that out?"

"There is only one interpretation that fits all the facts, once you know about his family's financial disaster, and that Electra is a rich epikleros. Kallias had been interested in Electra, but, because she is an epikleros, he wasn't sure whether it would be possible to marry her, because his father wouldn't let him be adopted by Electra's father. But now that they've lost their fortune, or almost all their fortune, it wasn't totally clear from what Kallisto was saying, his father positively wants him to be adopted by Electra's father, who is very rich; after all, he's already got another son and two grandsons. But Kallias thinks it would be dishonourable to do it now, when he wasn't prepared to do it when there were no financial considerations, though it hadn't been his fault, it was his father that wouldn't let him. But he obviously does care for Electra. That's it, I am sure that is the explanation, it fits everything we know."

"That's one possible explanation, sure, but you don't know

that it's the right one."

"No, I don't, but there must be some way to find out if I'm right." She thought for a bit and then her face lit up. "I know!"

"I'm not asking him any more questions, and that's final," Agias protested.

"You don't seem to have asked him any actual questions so far, as it happens, only what fell into your lap, but never mind, you did try, and you came up with the answers. Actually, I don't want you to ask anything this time, I just want you to tell him something, give him some information."

"What do you mean? What information?"

"That Electra has decided to marry her cousin after the festival."

"It's not true, I take it."

"No, of course it's not true. I just want to see how he reacts."

"And how am I going to find a way of telling him? I can't very well go up to him and say, 'Hi! Electra is going to marry her cousin'."

"Don't be silly. I'll tell you exactly how to do it. You'll say that you came to see me, and I sneaked out to meet you, give him a bit of detail about that, and then say how hectic things are at the sanctuary just now, give him a bit of gossip about the murders."

"What gossip? I don't know any gossip about the murders other than what everyone knows."

"Never mind, I'll tell you a few things to tell him. Now pay attention to the structure of what you'll say; after you've given him the gossip, then you'll say, 'Oh, yes, and one of Anthea's colleagues will be getting engaged after the festival, Electra, she apparently suddenly decided to agree to marry her cousin; she's an epikleros, you know.' You'll say exactly those words. Now

188

repeat them, so I know you took them in."

Agias did as instructed. Anthea corrected a minor deviation and made him repeat it again. Then she kissed him and he left, while she sneaked back into the amphipoleion.

Early the next morning Chloe attended the meeting at the mayor's house that Stephanos had arranged at her instigation, when he had received her letter in the middle of the night. When she got back from the meeting she had to deal with various organizational snags that had cropped up at the last minute, before she could go to supervise the bears' last crucial day of preparation.

When Chloe came outside and took over responsibility for the bears, and it was clear that the helpers weren't going to be needed for some time, Anthea dragged Electra away, behind a cluster of olive trees, leaving Helena to keep an eye on things and call them back if it became necessary. "I don't want to raise your hopes, because I may be wrong," she told Electra. "I may have misinterpreted the situation entirely, but ...this is what I think has been going on with Kallias." She explained everything that she had learnt, and her interpretations of what she knew. "So now," she concluded, "we have to wait and see how he reacts to what Agias will be telling him."

Electra was excited, elated, and also very scared. "It may be just wishful thinking," she said. "There are probably a lot of other explanations."

"I suppose there may be," Anthea admitted. "But I can't think of any, and this one fits all the facts."

"As far as we know them," Electra said. "Oh, I do so hope you are right."

"We'll soon know. Listen, the reason I told you now, before we know for sure, is because it occurred to me that Kallias may come and try to talk to you."

"Oh, no. I'd be terrified, I wouldn't know what to say."

"Look, if he comes to talk to you it would mean he loves you. Otherwise why bother? I mean, if Helena told me that a friend of her fiancé's is going to get engaged I wouldn't go and talk to him, would I? So if Kallias comes to talk to you we know he cares."

"But I wouldn't know what to say. And I can't lie."

"Uhmm …" Anthea pondered. "I think maybe if you are just yourself, flustered and tongue-tied, that might just do the trick." She smiled reassuringly, just as they heard Helena's low whistle, the signal that they were needed with the bears and had to get back.

The bears were about to begin a practice race, but just then Nikias appeared and asked Chloe's permission to have a quick word with his niece, Melissa. Chloe gave him permission and he led Melissa to the shade of a palm tree a bit further away, and started talking to her in an earnest but at the same time agitated way. The girls were staring, trying to make out what was going on, but Nikias had made sure that they were just out of earshot.

"Don't show anything, and don't look around. I've got some news to tell you, but you mustn't let them see that it's important, otherwise we'll both be in trouble afterwards. It's about Alexias."

"What is it? Has anything happened to him?" Melissa asked anxiously.

"I told you, don't show excitement, or anything, pretend it's nothing important."

"Will you tell me what's happened to Alexias, please, uncle?" Melissa's voice was unsteady.

"He's escaped from the mayor's house and he's leaving the country. He's asked me to say goodbye to you. He wanted you to know before you heard it from someone else, that he's run away. Unfortunately, he can't say goodbye to his mother, just to me and his sister, his mother is not coming back until tonight, and there isn't any time to lose. I bribed the guards and they let him go early this morning."

"Why, what's happened, why now?"

"I was told in confidence that there is new evidence against Alexias, or they understand some old evidence differently, I don't know, anyway, the thing is, they say that now he doesn't stand a chance."

"But he didn't do it. He's innocent. They can't do that," Melissa shouted, now visibly distraught.

"I'm afraid they can. You know he's innocent, and I know he's innocent, but it doesn't look as though we are going to be able to convince the jury, if we can't convince anyone else, and everyone believes that this new evidence clinches the matter. So, that's that. We can't risk it. He's got to go and never come back."

"No, no. He can't go. He can't go away. I've got to see him, where is he?"

"You can't see him, my dear. We don't want to attract anyone's attention. Anyway, he may have gone already, and if he hasn't he'll be leaving any minute. He was waiting to be fetched as soon as the small boat I hired from someone I trust arrives to take him away."

Melissa grabbed Nikias' arm and shook it. "I've got to see him. You've got to let me see him," she screamed.

Nikias disengaged his arm and stared at her. Then he said. "All right. If it means that much to you, I don't suppose it would do any harm. And you are attracting more attention now with these hysterics. If he's still there. He's hiding in a small farmhouse down the road. But I told you, he's probably gone already."

"How do I get there? Quick."

"I'll show you."

"No, no, just tell me, I've got to run. I've got to get there before he leaves."

"Well, you turn right at the North gatehouse and then go straight on until the end of the fig orchard."

"Is it the farm of the fig man?" Melissa interrupted him.

"Yes." Nikias sounded surprised.

Melissa took off running. She heard Chloe in the distance shouting "Melissa! Where do you think you are going? Come back here." But of course she paid no attention. She ran on, out of the sanctuary, down the road, through the orchards. She had to see Alexias before he left. She had to. She ran faster, until her breath was choking her. Eventually she reached the small farmhouse that belonged to the man she called 'the fig man', just a few rooms in an L-shaped arrangement that gave onto a yard on the inside; you couldn't see the yard from the road, you had to go through the gate and round the house to find it. That's where Alexias had been sitting, at a rough wooden table under climbing vines on a frame. When he heard someone coming he darted inside; Melissa ran after him, shouting "Alexias!!... come out, it's me Melissa, Alexias!!..."

Alexias came out again, looking thunderous. "What are you doing here, Melissa?" he said. "You aren't supposed to be here. Did anyone see you? Were you followed? You shouldn't have come."

"I had to see you. I have to stop you. You can't go away; you've got to stay here."

"Don't be stupid, I haven't got a choice. Do you think I want to go into exile, and never come back home? But I've got to go, otherwise I'll be prosecuted and convicted and put to death."

"No, no." Melissa screamed hysterically. "They can't do that. You didn't do it, you didn't kill them."

"Thanks for the vote of confidence, but that's not how

192

everyone else sees it, and they can most certainly put me to death, and that's why I've got to get away. And now you'd better leave, just in case the man who's coming to get me sees you and thinks it's not safe to come in." He turned as though to go inside the house.

Melissa grabbed his arm. "You can't go, you can't leave me." Alexias disengaged his arm and said, sternly, "Now you are being childish and you are starting to make a real nuisance of yourself."

"Don't say that. If you are going I want to come with you. Take me with you."

Alexias laughed. "Don't be silly, Melissa. As though I didn't have enough troubles already, without burdening myself with a child. What would I want to take you with me for?"

"I love you. In a couple of years we can get married. I love you more than anything, and I am not going to let you go."

Alexias burst into even louder laughter. "Don't be ridiculous. You love me, what do you know about love? You are just a silly child."

"Stop it! Don't keep calling me silly, and ridiculous, and childish."

"But that's what you are, a silly child. You don't understand anything about love or anything else. You are just a silly little girl."

"Don't say that!"

"Why not? It's true."

"It's not true, I love you, please take me with you. Please."

"There you are, you see, you are being silly again. You don't love me, it's just a childish fancy, you'll get over it before the month is over."

"It's not true!! It's not true!!" She screamed and tried to throw herself at him. "I love you. I killed them for you!"

"What? What did you just say?"

"Ah, that surprised you, didn't it? I told you I am not a child. And I told you I love you."

"What did you mean, you killed them for me?"

"I killed Daphne. I heard her telling you that she was pregnant, and that you had to marry her, when you met her in the porch of the amphipoleion the night before the Sacred Hunt. And I heard you arrange to meet her at the Hunt. I wasn't going to let her ruin your life. So I made sure I wasn't going to be the one impersonating the goddess by shooting badly in the second round, and then when we went off after Kallisto, I sneaked away into the woods and went to the place where she was waiting for you, and I hit her on the head with a large stone. When she saw me coming it didn't cross her mind to worry; she just told me to go away, she was waiting for someone. She thought, like everyone else, that I had a crush on her. In fact I was keeping an eye on her because I knew you thought you fancied her and she was after you. And just as well I did, otherwise I wouldn't have found out about the baby and that she was trying to get you to marry her."

"But I loved Daphne. I wanted to marry her."

"And I love you. And I knew that if I got rid of her you'd come to love me eventually, and marry me when I grew up a bit more, as your father wanted. Anyway, the child wasn't yours."

"You didn't know that then. None of us did."

"Daphne did. But it didn't make any difference anyway, whose it was. I wasn't going to let her ruin your life, and take you away from me."

"Did you kill Philippos as well?"

"Yes, of course I did."

"But why?"

"Isn't it obvious? I wanted to make it clear to everyone that

194

you hadn't killed Daphne, since the same person would have killed both, and you were under guard in the mayor's house."

"You killed Philippos to give me an alibi?"

"Yes, of course. I never thought that they would arrest you for Daphne's murder, it was a terrible shock, well, it was a terrible shock finding you cradling her body in the first place, that's when I started getting worried, and they arrested you, and I didn't know what to do. And then the next day I was walking to the beach on my own, thinking about it, and Philippos jumped out of a vineyard and asked me to go in the vineyard with him and kiss him; he's been after me for ages, that's when I realized there was an easy solution: I would kill him, and then everyone would assume that the same person killed both him and Daphne and that this person couldn't be you. So I found a largish stone with sharp edges and I said I'd go in the vineyard with him, and I did, and I killed him. I thought they would let you go after that, when they found the body."

The door behind Melissa, which had been ajar, burst wide open, and Stephanos stepped out. "So Chloe was right," he said, as Andron, Charias, and the mayor of Philaidai came out into the yard after him. "It was Melissa. I couldn't really believe it."

"I couldn't believe it either," Andron said. "I don't know if I would have quite believed it ever, if I hadn't heard it with my own ears. I have to admit that I would never have agreed to this scheme if you hadn't twisted my arm," he said to Stephanos; and then, to Alexias, "Well done, Alexias, you played your part magnificently."

Melissa's initial bewildered shock exploded into fury. "How could you do this to me?" she screamed at Alexias, pummelling him with her fists. "I did it for you, I did it because I love you, and you betrayed me."

"No, Melissa." Chloe, who had just walked into the yard,

contradicted her. "You didn't do it for Alexias, you did it for yourself. Because you wanted him, and you didn't want to lose him, either to Daphne or to a murder conviction."

Melissa spat at Chloe. Then she darted between the men's legs and tried to run away; but her way was blocked by three large slaves belonging to Andron. They took her by the wrists while they waited for Andron to decide what to do next. "We'll take her to your house," he said to the mayor, "and summon her parents."

After Melissa had been taken away, and the others began to follow, Alexias turned on Chloe. "My mother is right," he hissed. "You are a self-righteous prig. Couldn't you have left her that little consolation, that she did it for love?"

"No, I couldn't, as it happens. I don't know what's going to happen to her, but whatever happens, she'll need to change the way she sees the world, realize that it doesn't revolve round her, and other people aren't just pawns for her self-gratification; and letting her cocoon herself in flattering fictions is not going to help her do it. Believe me, she doesn't need more self-esteem, she needs less. And so do you. I wasn't expecting thanks from you, but mild politeness would have been appropriate, don't you think, considering what would have happened to you if it hadn't been for me?" She turned her back on him and followed Stephanos and the others to the house of the mayor of Philaidai.

When they arrived at the mayor's house Nikias and Alexias withdrew and went to wait for Melissa's parents on their own in another room. It's not exactly that they were ambivalent about what had happened, they weren't, they were relieved that it was all over and Alexias was safe; Nikias of course was also relieved that his son wouldn't be marrying a pregnant girlfriend, and pregnant by someone else, what's more, as Nikias had guessed, his own uncle, as it turned out. But they did feel some guilt that it had been their actions, and the lies they told, that had tricked Nikias' brother's ten year old daughter.

"But Chloe was right," Alexias said, as though his father had been arguing with him. "She did kill Daphne. And poor Philippos."

The mayor had taken his other guests to his main reception room. He offered them some fruit and wine and then he and Stephanos asked Chloe to explain how she had come to the conclusion that Melissa was the killer.

Chloe had been blaming herself for being slow. "There were a lot of things that should have made me realize much earlier that Melissa was the killer," she said, "but there's some sort of mental block about suspecting a girl who is not quite ten years old yet. If I had been quicker maybe Philippos would still be alive – though I suppose by that stage there hadn't been that much to go on."

"Come on!" Stephanos objected. "You can't blame yourself for being slow, when the rest of us didn't see it at all. Tell us how you did realize that Melissa was the killer."

"It all slotted into place in my mind while I was asleep. Some would say that the goddess sent me the inspiration, like a vision. But once I thought of Melissa as a possibility, everything fitted, and it was the only explanation that fitted everything we knew. She had the opportunity to kill both Daphne and Philippos. She was in the woods with Kallisto and the other hunters, and we know that they were separated. I should have realized that she was in a position to know that Daphne was going to be at the stream waiting for Kallias, because I knew that she had been out roaming about the night before, when Kallisto thought she was in the orchards stealing figs, so she could have seen Daphne and Kallias meet in the outer porch of the amphipoleion and gone over to listen. That would explain how she knew that Daphne was threatening her dream of marrying Alexias."

"That's what she said to Alexias, that she heard Daphne telling him that she was having his baby, and Alexias saying that he would marry her. And that she heard them arrange to meet the next morning at the Hunt, and where. But it was obviously not a coincidence that she saw them, she told Alexias that she had been watching Daphne because she knew Alexias fancied her; if she'd seen her taking wine to the other girls and to Mego she would have known she was up to something and followed her."

"That sounds right." Chloe agreed. "The other thing that struck me as blindingly obvious in retrospect, once I thought of her at all, was the question of the blood. Even if her clothes had been spattered with blood when she killed Daphne she could have had a superficial wash in the brook, and anything else would have been covered up by the stag's blood when she rejoined the others, she would have made sure they didn't have a close look before she helped manhandle the stag. Anyone who saw blood on her would have assumed it was the stag's blood. It would have been even easier with Philippos, since he had been trying to get her on her own, poor lad. That's probably what gave her the idea. She must have been going to the beach early on her own, and Philippos managed to waylay her somewhere where no one could see them, and she took the opportunity to kill him. She then swam into the sea wearing her saffron robe to wash away any blood and rejoined us. When challenged about swimming in her robe she invented a man looking at her in a funny way. And then when Alexias wasn't released, and she thought her plan wasn't working, she put the anonymous letter she'd stolen from Daphne's chest in Helena's chest to throw suspicion on Electra."

"Why had she stolen the letter in the first place, do you think? She surely wasn't thinking that far ahead."

"No, no. I think she'd searched Daphne's chest to be on the safe side, either before we'd left for the Hunt or immediately when the bears got back, when there was total confusion – not that there could have been anything incriminating, the poor fool never thought that Melissa was anything other than her devoted slave; and she found the letter and she thought she'd keep it just in case. It gave her some sort of power over Electra, and Melissa loved having power over people. And that's another thing, her personality, it fitted perfectly the personality I thought the murderer would have. And the motive was there once you looked for it. And I still didn't see it."

"You did in the end. And you found a way of proving what sounded incredible to the rest of us."

"Alexias must have played his role very convincingly. And Nikias."

"Oh, yes," Stephanos said. "They were both amazing. Mind you, once Melissa thought things were going wrong, she lost her cool and eventually became hysterical, and by that time she wouldn't have noticed anything amiss, unless Alexias took out a script and started reading from it. But they did act well. Nothing like the idea that Alexias' life was in the balance to motivate both of them."

"Is that what you told him? That his life was in danger? That you would prosecute him and he would be convicted unless…" The mayor of Philaidai sounded censorious.

"Yes, sure, that's what I told them. That this was their only chance, and it was up to them to make it work. They needed to be motivated, and they were."

"But you lied," the mayor said. "It's bad enough having a conspiracy of adults to trick a ten year old, but to do it on the basis of lies as well…"

"Oh, I see, so you think it would have been better to let a

killer go free and unrecognized to kill again, and, incidentally, to pollute the rites, and for Alexias to have suspicion hanging over his head for the rest of his life, as long as we did no tricking, and I told no lies. I'm sorry, but that's not how I see things. If I have to tell a few lies to get justice, and to stop a killer from killing more people in the future, it doesn't worry me."

"But justice is about rules; if you bend the rules, where will it end? You become as bad as the people you are trying to catch."

"Oh, no, you are wrong there. Yes, we need rules to get justice, but justice is not about the rules. If you are telling me that unless we are slaves to the rules, unless the rules become an end in themselves, there's going to be anarchy and anomie, it's a sad indictment of the human race, and I don't believe you. And if you are telling me that bending the rules to get justice is as bad as killing innocent people, then it's a sad indictment of you, of the confusion your sort of thinking can lead to. It's not difficult to see what is just and what isn't, and…"

He was interrupted by a loud wailing. Melissa's parents had arrived. Leandros was pale and rigid on his litter, while Hermione was wailing uncontrollably. When Nikias and Alexias joined them, Leandros asked his brother, "Is it certain that she did it?"

"I am afraid it is," Nikias said, placing a hand on his brother's shoulder. "She confessed to Alexias, in the hearing of several other people."

"She may have been making it up, to attract attention. You know what kids are like."

"I'm afraid she wasn't making it up. I am very sorry, Leandros, but it is the truth." He put his arms around his brother's shoulders, squeezed them and then moved away.

"Oh, goddess above, where did we go wrong?" cried

Hermione in distress. "We always did our best for her; we always told her how much we love her, and we cherished her, and we always tried to give her everything she wanted."

'That's your answer then,' thought Chloe, 'she came to feel entitled, and if other people were in the way, too bad for them.' Of course, not being a cruel person, she said nothing. She put her arm around Hermione and took her to the room where Melissa was waiting, furious at being tricked and caught, and vowing revenge.

Chapter Twenty-Seven

"Melissa! I cannot believe it!" Anthea screeched, but then she corrected herself. "Well, no, actually, I can. That girl was always so selfish and insensitive, so …horrible."

"I know what you mean." Electra agreed. "She feels entitled to have everything she wants, everything the way she likes it. But she's not quite ten yet, and actually to kill …to hit another human being with a stone again and again until they are dead. Two human beings."

When Chloe had given the news to the three helpers, that it had been Melissa who had killed Daphne and Philippos, they had gone rigid with shock. But gradually, they started talking it through.

"She's a monster," Helena said. "A real human monster."

"Oh, come on," Anthea was a little scornful. "As Electra said, she's very very young. She's not a nice person, as we all know, but to call a young child a monster is a bit hysterical."

"Actually, I agree with Helena," Electra said. "I think she is a monster. Like Daphne, she thought she was entitled to whatever she wanted, at whatever cost to other people. Daphne didn't kill anyone, but she was prepared to ruin poor Alexias' life for her own convenience. I think people like that are a class apart."

"You aren't saying they are all monsters, surely."

"Maybe they don't all end up as monsters, but they have the potential."

Chloe was surprised to hear the firmness in Electra's voice. But then, of course, one forgot that it was self-confidence that Electra lacked, not confidence in her own opinions. And for good reason. She was a very intelligent girl, and very well read.

"Everyone has the potential," Anthea said.

"That's rubbish! That's just what people say because they want to pretend there is little difference between cold-blooded killers and the rest of us. We may all be in danger of doing some sort of wrong in certain circumstances, but only people who think they are entitled to whatever they want at whatever cost to others have the potential for cold-blooded murder. And they are a group apart."

"Are you saying that these people are born evil?"

"Partly born and partly made, I should think, a combination of the two. But that's not the important point; the important point is that once they are 'made' they can't be unmade."

"If that's what you think, what would you do with them?" Anthea asked.

"People who think they are entitled to whatever they want and they have crossed the line to get it? I would write them off, in one way or another."

"You mean kill them. Even youngsters like Melissa."

"Not necessarily, though in fact that is the most logical thing, the best protection for the weak and the innocent, which is why the city puts to death those guilty of serious crimes. Because it is the weak and the innocent that are the monsters' real victims."

"Daphne was neither innocent nor weak."

"No," Electra said, "but Philippos was."

"So what would you do with them?" Anthea returned to her question. "You didn't say."

"I would put them all on an island, and guard the coastline

all around it, so that they can't escape, and let them build their own community, rather than batten on the rest of us. If they learn to live as socialized human beings, they would be all right. If not, not. It would be their choice."

"But that's cruel. We are civilized people."

"I happen to think that it's much less civilized to expose the weak to whatever savage people want to do to whoever stands in the way of whatever they want, money, pleasure, whatever; you think it's more civilized not to hurt the savage people, and have the old and the weak live in fear and die in violence? Why? Because you aren't involved? You let them suffer by default, at the hands of others? Because that's what happens if the city doesn't cut off such people from the rest of us. If a society ever comes to put the rights of the predators above those of the weak and the vulnerable, it won't be a civilized society, it will be a cruel and deluded one, and it will rot from the inside."

"Why should any society do that?"

"Well, they wouldn't necessarily be thinking they were doing it. They would be thinking that they were giving the predators the same rights as anyone else, because, like you, they'd think that it is the humane and civilized thing to do. But if you follow that to its natural conclusion, you'd end up by privileging the predators."

"I don't see how."

"Well, first of all, if you are so obsessive about the rights of the predators it becomes more difficult to catch them and punish them; and there are a lot more innocent victims as a result. So the predators' rights take priority over the right of the innocent not to be killed or beaten up or robbed. Then, let's suppose that what has just happened here had happened in the sort of society I am talking about. Because Melissa is so young, they would probably treat her very gently, and look after her, and if any

204

member of Daphne's family wanted to inflict a proper punishment, kill her, or whatever, the city would have to devote resources to protecting Melissa, and hounding the victims' family – instead of protecting old men and women who are being beaten up and robbed. And, what does this tell the predators, and what does it tell those who are neither predators nor virtuous people, but could go either way?"

"You've obviously been reading your father's philosophy books and utopias, or dystopias, rather, in this case."

"I've been reading some, and I've been trying to write one as well."

"Really?" Anthea sounded astonished. "Why didn't you tell me?"

"Because you would have made fun of me, as you are doing now."

"No, I am not making fun of you; I just don't see the point of bothering with all that. Neither you nor I have got a vote in the Assembly, or a political voice. So what's the point?"

"And you disagree with my views."

"What worries me is that you talk as though there were the good people on one side and the bad ones on the other. While I think all of us have elements of both."

"There you go again. It doesn't matter if we all have elements of good and bad, what matters are the choices we make. And the choices many people make are affected by the way they see the city dealing with wrongdoing. Also, as I said, I do think that people who think they are entitled to what they want and have crossed the line to get it, are different from the rest of us."

"But Melissa is so young."

"And you think that someone like that can change as she grows up? People like Daphne and Melissa, who only see their own desires, and have no feelings whatsoever for anyone else? I don't think so. Maybe Melissa will learn to manage it better, this perversion she has, but if she gets the chance she'll do it again, or something else like it."

"What a bleak view of the world you've got."

"On the contrary, it's you who's got the bleak view of the world, because you think we are basically all bad. I think most, or at least many, people aren't; maybe they are not perfect, but they wouldn't assume their convenience rates higher than other people's lives, or even rights, like with Daphne and Alexias. And there are a lot of people in-between who may turn bad if they see that badness pays."

"If you've all finished," Chloe broke into their conversation, "I think we should go and talk to the bears now."

It had been decided that they would not tell the bears the truth about Melissa and the murders until after the festival was over. It would have been too upsetting for them to come to terms with it, and at the same time cope successfully with the stress of the festival. And this was really important for the rest of their lives – and for the city, of course. So Chloe told them that Melissa had fallen down and hurt herself when she had run away that morning, that she had broken a leg, and so she would not be taking part in the festival, and that she had been taken to stay with her parents, at her parents' friend's house. As she hadn't been a popular child, no one cared very much. Only Thekla said, "Good riddance to bad rubbish …she always thought she could get away with anything, just because her uncle is the priestess' husband."

"That's not a very charitable thing to say," Anthea said, and she meant it; if an innocent Melissa had broken her leg, that would have been a horrible thing to say, she felt.

"Then it's just the right thing for Melissa," Zoe responded, in support of her friend, "Melissa is not a very charitable person."

They then forgot about Melissa, and went on to practise singing hymns. Of course, the sanctuary had to be purified, since Melissa, a polluted murderer, had been freely living in it, and moving about everywhere, though fortunately there had been no call for her to approach the altar, or go into the temple and approach the goddess' statue. But the sanctuary as a whole had to be purified, and all those who had been in contact with her, which included the bears. As they had no idea what ritual activities took place just before the festival, they believed what they were told, that this was part of the normal procedure. Three piglets were sacrificed to purify the sanctuary; their throats were cut over the altar, and their blood was spilled all over the sanctuary, and then their corpses were carried around the sanctuary's boundaries. More piglets were sacrificed over the altar in the rite that purified the bears and the helpers, as well as the subpriestess and the slaves involved with the bears, who were all sprinkled with the piglets' blood.

It was still light when the procession arrived from the city. Theano was at its head, carrying the ancient wooden statue. Various magistrates and other officials, and the priests and priestesses of other major Athenian cults, marched behind her in the official part of the procession. There was a large crowd of people following, men, women and children; some of the men appeared to be drunk – the walk from Athens was long, and a lot of wine had been consumed on the way. Eventually the pilgrims would put up tents all around the sanctuary.

The procession was received at the entrance of the sanctuary with music, hymns and dances performed by the bears. Then more hymns were sung by choruses of adolescent virgins, who had come in the procession from the city, and who had themselves been bears – which is where they had received their choral training. After that a goat was sacrificed at the altar. The sacrificial animal was taken to the altar in a procession, accompanied by attendants, a flute player, and the priestess Theano. This procession was, as always, led by a virgin of marriageable age who carried the sacrificial basket, called 'kanephoros'. It was a very great honour to be a kanephoros, especially at a major city festival like the Brauronia – an honour for the girl, and also for her family. Theano had chosen Daphne to be the kanephoros at the Brauronia, but after Daphne's death, and the embarrassing revelation that, far from being a virgin, she was in fact pregnant, Theano had left the choice of her replacement to Chloe. Chloe had chosen Electra.

Anthea had been rather annoyed to begin with, but then she said to Helena, "She needs this much more than we do. It will please her father and maybe make him more amenable to her pleas, and also maybe it will give Kallias a push, if he sees her beautifully dressed and the centre of everyone's attention, maybe he'll feel irresistibly attracted, and decide to do something about it." Electra did indeed look beautiful, in her patterned, brightly coloured, dress and cloak, holding the sacrificial basket on her head, in a pose that flattered her figure and made her look highly desirable.

The procession circled the altar, then they stopped and ritually washed their hands, and Theano dipped a torch in the lustral water and sprinkled the altar and the goat, which shook as it was sprinkled, signifying that it was consenting to its sacrifice. For it is the Greek custom not to sacrifice before assent is signalled by the animal. Then, Theano took up barley grains from the sacrificial basket and threw them on the animal and on the altar, and after a brief ritual silence, she prayed to Artemis, and cut off a few hairs from the goat's head and threw them into the fire, consecrating the victim to the goddess. Then its throat was drawn back and cut over the altar, while the women raised a shrill cry. The blood was collected in a bowl, and poured on the altar. After the animal was skinned Theano placed the gods' share on the altar to be burnt, while the assistants roasted the innards, the liver, spleen, heart, lungs, kidneys, over the fire on forks. The rest of the meat was boiled and would be eaten by those entitled to have a share.

That evening the various magistrates and other officials, and the priests and priestesses of the other Athenian cults, and, of course, Theano, Chloe and Mego, dined in the dining room suites in the porticoed building to the North of the temple. Other pilgrims, whose status was not quite so high, but were nevertheless of some importance, dined in the open air court that was enclosed on three sides by the wings of the porticoed building. The rest ate in the open air all over the sanctuary.

The festivities went on all night. The helpers were supposed to make sure that the bears behaved themselves and got enough sleep before their big day tomorrow, but after they had seen them all to bed the girls had gone outside to sit on the porch of the amphipoleion, expecting Bakchis and the other slaves to keep an eye on things inside. Clearly, that eye was not all that close, for some time after the bears were supposed to be asleep in their beds the helpers saw Kallisto outside, walking towards them; she came up to Electra and said, "My brother Kallias wants to see you. He's waiting for you over there under the olive tree."

"What?" Electra shrieked.

"My brother Kallias wants to see you. He's waiting for you over there under the olive tree," Kallisto repeated.

"Yes, she heard you the first time, thank you," Anthea said. "'What' was just an expression of surprise."

"Oh, I see. Well, anyway, are you going to go or what? I've got to go back and tell him."

"Yes, she'll be coming in a minute," Anthea said. "Go and tell him. And then go back to bed. I'll be watching you."

When Kallisto left, Anthea turned to Electra and told her "You are going, don't even think about not going."

"No, no, I can't, I wouldn't know what to do."

"You are going to talk to him if Helena and I have to drag you there. Think of how humiliating that's going to be."

"But what am I going to say to him?"

"You don't have to say anything. He asked to see you, let him speak first."

"I can't do it."

"Yes, you can. I am not going to let you throw your life away. If you don't go now, and you then marry someone who means nothing to you, and you have a small, limiting life, you are going to regret this night to the end of your days. So we are going to drag you there if necessary. One way or another you are going to talk to Kallias tonight."

"But he may not want to say what you think he does. It may be something to do with Kallisto."

"If it isn't what I think it is, then it isn't. At least we'll know. And you'll know that you did your best."

Eventually Electra, reluctant and eager at the same time, walked in the direction Kallisto had indicated and disappeared among the olive trees. When she eventually came back she was shining in the dark. "He does love me!" she said. She hugged Anthea wildly. "He wants to marry me." He is prepared to have himself adopted by my father." When she went up to him, she told Anthea and Helena, Kallias had asked her if it was true that she was going to marry her cousin, and she didn't know what to say, because she remembered Anthea had told her not to deny it,

210

but she didn't want to lie, so she did what came natural to her anyway, following Anthea's instructions, she blushed and stammered incoherently. Kallias then had started shouting that she couldn't do that, that he loved her, and he had thought she wasn't indifferent to him, from the glances they had exchanged over the last few months. And then Electra forgot to be shy and scared, and she got a bit angry, and she told him that she had thought she had been mistaken, since he had cut her dead when they came face to face at the Sacred Hunt. Kallias then told her the whole story. He said that before, when they had first met, he had liked her, more than liked her, he started feeling she was the girl he wanted to marry. But when he found out that she was an epikleros, and he talked to his father about it, and his father told him that he was not going to allow him to be adopted into another family, and that it would be foolish to contract a marriage knowing that it could, at least in theory, be terminated by one of her father's relatives. It's true that it was unlikely that the court would decide to break up a marriage these days, but you never know, and it wasn't worth taking the risk. "So, I was rather confused," he said. "I was really attracted to you a lot, and kept thinking about you, but…"

"But what?"

"I didn't know if what I felt was worth my fighting with my father – even if I knew that you wanted to marry me, and that your father was prepared to adopt me, which I didn't."

"So what has changed?"

He told her that everything had changed, that the situation had been turned on its head when his elder brother had ruined them financially, or virtually ruined them. After that his father had changed his attitude entirely, he now positively wanted Kallias to be adopted by Electra's father and marry Electra, so that what was left of his household's wealth wouldn't have to be divided between him and his brother. But Kallias thought it would be dishonourable to do it now, when it was financially advantageous to them, when they weren't prepared to do it before.

"So, if you think it's so dishonourable, what are you doing here, telling me you want to marry me?"

"I don't care if it is dishonourable. I can't bear the idea of you marrying someone else, so honour or not, I want to marry you. If you want me that is."

"And then we kissed," Electra concluded, and it was just… I've never felt anything like this."

"What about your father? Is he going to agree to all this, the marriage and the adoption?" Helena asked.

"Well, I'll find out tomorrow. But that's the least of my worries. If Kallias loves me that's all that matters."

"In an ideal world," Helena said. "As it is, if I were you, I'd use all my wiles on my father tomorrow."

"But I haven't got any wiles," Electra protested.

"Never mind," Anthea said thoughtfully. "We'll think of something."

The next day was the main day of the festival. In the morning several bards recited passages from Homer's *Iliad*, while most of the afternoon was dedicated to the ritual that ended the girls' service as bears. First, the girls performed dances and they sang hymns and eventually, one by one, they shed the saffron robe that symbolized their service as bears in front of the altar, and stood naked. Each ran round the altar, and then, still naked, one by one, they lined up for the race. Eventually Theano gave a command and they started running. It was a longish course, and it became clear very soon that one girl was consistently at the front. It was Kallisto, and she won the race. Theano crowned her with a palm wreath, and then Chloe led the bears away, Kallisto on her own at the front. Her victory at the race meant that she was graduating as leader of the bears, and one with special distinction, since she had also won the shooting competition at the Sacred Hunt and had impersonated Artemis. After an interval, the girls returned, again led by Kallisto, wearing new grown-up clothes, and with their hair gathered up in a roll at the back of their head, to signify that they were no longer children, but were (relatively) soon to become marriageable virgins. They performed a dance in their new clothes and then their service to the goddess was over.

Afterwards, the city, the girls' families and other private individuals offered sacrifices of cattle and sheep. The meat from the city sacrifices was distributed to the pilgrims, and the individuals who had performed their own sacrifices shared the meat with their friends. Whatever their financial situation, Kallisto's father had to sacrifice a sheep to celebrate the completion of his daughter's service as a bear, especially since she had graduated as leader of the bears. Everyone tried to be as cheerful as possible for Kallisto's sake, especially her grandmother. Kallisto was very proud of her granddaughter, who was named after her, and she wished that her friend Praxilla could have been here to share in her joy, but she knew that it wasn't appropriate. Praxilla was no longer excluded from the sanctuary as a polluted mourner, that period was over, but this was a joyful occasion, and it wouldn't have been right for her to come – at least this is what she had said to Kallisto, when Kallisto had suggested the possibility. 'It's not that I am heartbroken exactly', Praxilla had said. 'Not as I would have been if Stephanos had died. But it's just not right.'

Kallisto noticed that her younger grandson Kallias was jumpy and restless and something else she couldn't quite identify. 'Something is going on', she thought. 'I wonder whether he's changed his mind about the girl.' So she called him over and asked him, and eventually, after Kallias realized that his grandmother was not going to accept his assurances that everything was fine and leave him alone, he told her how things stood, and that it was now up to Electra's father, and that he, Kallias, was worried that Electra's father was going to want Electra to marry his brother's son. Kallisto thought for a bit and then said, "Electra, your Electra's paternal grandmother, we were bears together; she was a year younger than Praxilla and me, but still, we were bears together. Do you know if she's here at the festival?"

"I don't know. Do you want me to find out?"

"Yes, and find out where they are sitting, but don't let them see you yet."

When Kallias came back he reported that there was an elderly lady in Electra's party, but he didn't know whether she was Electra's paternal grandmother.

"Never mind," Kallisto said. "Let's walk in that direction and we'll see."

When they approached Electra's family Kallisto saw that the elderly lady Kallias had mentioned was indeed Electra senior. She went up to her, saying, as though surprised, "It is Electra, isn't it? You do remember me, Kallisto, we were bears together. My granddaughter Kallisto was the leader of the bears today."

"Yes, of course I remember you; many congratulations for your granddaughter. You must be very proud. My granddaughter Electra was one of the helpers, and she was also the kanephoros at the goat sacrifice." She paused, then asked, "You were a friend of Praxilla's weren't you? The dead girl's aunt. And the boy's."

"Yes," Kallisto said. "You have an excellent memory."

214

"How is Praxilla? Is she totally distraught?"

Kallisto thought and then said. "Distraught enough. She couldn't of course come to the festival. She must be feeling pretty low just now. I was thinking of visiting her, cheering her up a bit."

'That's news to me', Kallias thought, while trying to signal to Electra not to worry about his sudden appearance with his grandmother.

"I'll come with you if you like," Electra's grandmother offered. "We can take our carriage."

'Yes!' Kallisto thought, as they set off towards the gate. After they had spoken a little about the murders, and about Praxilla, Kallisto said, "My grandson Kallias is in love with your granddaughter Electra, and she is in love with him."

Electra laughed. "I knew there was more to your turning up than just chance and the desire to reminisce. Tell me about it." After Kallisto had told Electra everything she knew, Electra was silent for a while. Then she said very firmly. "As far as I am concerned, Electra's happiness is much more important than Charias' desire to increase his wealth – that's assuming that this is what he's got in mind, and we don't know that yet, but I suspect it is, because he's been hanging around recently. If so, he and his father, my younger son, would have been trying to influence Electra's father, who is a bit of an intellectual, not very wise in the ways of the world. And they would know what buttons to push. I have to handle this very carefully. Come on, let's get back. I'll let you know as soon as I have some news."

So the two elderly ladies did not go to visit Praxilla, but returned to their families, one to wait, the other to start her campaign to convince her son to do the right thing.

Eventually, the festival was over. 'Well, that's it for another few years', Chloe thought. 'Back to reality.' Most of the pilgrims were staying the night in their tents, drinking through the night in many cases; they would be starting the trip back to the city, or whatever place each had come from, the next morning. Tonight the official guests were being entertained by Theano; she gave a private banquet for the official guests at every festival, but this was the first time that Chloe had also been invited.

Theano was glowing. Her brother may have been disgraced, but her son was totally cleared and he was back at Rhamnous training with his unit. No doubt he would have to submit to some quite heavy punishment for leaving without permission, something painful or humiliating, or both, but it would be short term, and his life was all ahead of him, free of encumbrances once again. Obviously, Chloe thought, in Theano's eyes her brother's disgrace was a price worth paying for her son's freedom, hence her own invitation to the banquet. After all, Leon had brought it all on himself. 'And for all I know she may have resented his arrogance and the high-handed way he treated her all these years; of course, she wouldn't have dared acknowledge it, even to herself, but now …there's probably an element of pleasure in her reaction. And who can blame her?'

Chloe had gone to the banquet expecting Stephanos to be there, but he wasn't. 'Just as well', she told herself. 'What's the point? I am not going to see him again, and it's for the best. One can make a complete fool of oneself with fantasies, and I'm not a young girl to be able to live it down if I do. If he knew how I felt I would be a laughing stock, and I would lose what little I've got, my reputation, such as it has been since my father's death.'

She left the banquet as soon as it was decent to do so. As she was walking to her quarters in the amphipoleion, the stars and the moon were shining in a bright sky, and the smells of jasmine and honeysuckle made her feel dizzy. 'He made me feel alive again, for some reason', she thought; 'it's like my body is buzzing and my blood is jumping when I think of him, though he never touched me – and he would probably be revolted by the very idea. I'll just let this live in my head for a little longer, and then it will die a slow, gradual, death, and I will be back to being my usual self. It's not as though I am ever likely to see him again.'

When she reached her quarters she found that she had a visitor. Electra's father had been waiting to see her for some time. Chloe ushered him into her sitting room and asked him to sit down. When he did, he seemed reluctant to speak. Eventually, he said, "I have a strange request to make of you. I want to ask you what will seem a very odd question, and I would be very very grateful if you would answer me honestly, not that I am suggesting that you would lie, but you may feel you should be tactful or at least diplomatic. I would be extremely grateful if you would just tell me the honest truth as you see it, and then I will explain why I am asking you."

"Fine, go ahead, ask me."

"What do you think of my daughter Electra?"

"I beg your pardon?"

"What is your opinion of my daughter Electra? How would you assess her personality? Please, tell me what you really think. It's very important. I promise to explain everything."

"I think that she is a very good person; she is honest, loyal, straightforward and extremely bright. She is very sensitive, which is good in one way, but which can make her miserable as well, because not everyone around her is as sensitive as her, and sometimes she finds it difficult to handle that. And she doesn't have much self-confidence."

"So you don't think she's full of herself and manipulative?"

Chloe laughed. "No, of course I don't, in fact the exact opposite. Why? Is that what you think? That Electra is full of herself and manipulative?"

"No, I don't, but I wanted to make sure."

"Would you tell me what this is about? I would probably be able to be of more help to you if I knew what was going on."

"My mother just told me that Electra is in love with a young man, Kallias, the son of Kallimachos, the brother of the leader of the bears, and he is in love with her. She, my mother, had just found out the whole story from the young man's grandmother, that his father had not wanted him to be adopted into another family, as he would have to be if he were to marry my daughter, to safeguard the marriage, and that they then lost their money, and his father changed his mind and wanted him to be adopted out, but the young man thought it was dishonourable, and how in the end he decided he loved Electra too much and he wanted to marry her."

Chloe felt elated. "Oh, I am so pleased that he loves her too." she said. "I knew she had feelings for him, but I didn't know how he felt about her."

"So you approve?"

"As I told you, Electra is a very sensitive girl. She can be very happy or very unhappy. Happiness cannot be guaranteed, but she will definitely be unhappy unless she marries someone she loves, and who loves her, and who would respect her as a person. And it's obvious, just from this story, that Kallias does both."

"You don't think then that she needs a strong man's hand to guide her, and that once she is made to accept the husband I choose for her she will settle and be contented?"

"I don't think you believe that, do you?"

"I just wanted to make sure."

"May I guess that what you just said is not your own view, but something someone else suggested to you?"

"My brother and my nephew."

"And you believed them?"

"Not really, I know my nephew wants to marry Electra, and he would say anything to put me off letting her choose for herself, but they …they said I was being soft, and that I had always spoiled her – which isn't true, what I did is respect her opinions, which I know not every father of daughters does, but it's not spoiling, and I don't believe that all women necessarily need a strong guiding hand. Only, drip drip drip, it makes you come to doubt yourself. Until my mother spoke to me, and made me see that they are wrong. But I did want some confirmation, which is why I came to see you."

"I am delighted if I was able to help, but I think you had decided already. I think you know your daughter, and you trust your mother more than you trust your brother and your nephew."

He laughed. "But you did give me the reassurance I needed just now, before I make my decision known to the family. We'll announce the engagement immediately, and I'll start proceedings to adopt Kallias as soon as possible."

The next morning, after everything had been arranged between the men, the two families got together for an informal celebration; Electra and the young Kallisto embraced each other in an ecstatic hug. It would have been improper for Electra and Kallias to embrace, so in a way Electra felt that she was also hugging Kallias through Kallisto. Kallisto was just happy. "We'll be sisters," she said, again and again. "Wait till I tell Eunice. She'll be green with envy!"

Later that morning Bakchis came to tell Chloe that her brother Melanthios had just arrived and wanted to see her. Chloe was worried. What was her brother doing here? There must be something wrong with their mother, but why hadn't he sent a message, instead of coming all this way? Unless she was dead.

Melanthios was about forty, of medium height and build, with brown hair and brown eyes. When she saw him come in Chloe realized that he didn't look sad, let alone bereaved. He looked happy, and he was smiling.

"Is anything the matter?" Chloe asked. "I wasn't expecting to see you here."

"I wasn't expecting to be here myself. But I bring good news." A ripple of doubt crossed his face as he looked at her intensely. "At least I hope it's good news."

"Tell me."

Now that it came to telling her he seemed to become uncertain. "You know I am your legal guardian."

"I am not likely to forget, am I? Sorry, I didn't mean to sound hostile, it's not about you. But you know how I feel about the situation."

"Well anyway, it was the proper thing to do to come to me about it, though, of course, it isn't a matter of permission, it's just the way things are done. It is entirely up to you and I made that perfectly clear." He stopped, and then went on. "I have received a request for your hand in marriage, though, as I said, he made it clear, and I made it clear to him, that it wasn't exactly a request, just going through the proper channels. It's you who decides. I am not a barbarian."

"No, of course you are not. Are you going to tell me who it is who wants to marry me?"

"Oh, I thought you'd guess, I thought there may have been some sort of understanding, but I wasn't sure."

Chloe was trying to stop herself from thinking, let alone hoping. So she concentrated on Melanthios, and she realized that he was very nervous, that he was desperately hoping that the proposal would be to her liking; and it finally hit her, what it must be like for him, a man of very moderate means, and without influence, to be carrying the responsibility for her and their mother, the widow and the daughter of a man convicted of treason, the unmarried awkward daughter of a traitor, all these years; and he had never said anything to suggest it was a burden. Suddenly she was very touched.

"It's Stephanos, the son of Satyros from Melite."

Chloe burst into tears, and sobs she could not control. Melanthios took her in his arms and told her that she didn't have to accept the proposal if she didn't want to, he had assumed that she would want to, but it was up to her. "We don't need him, or his money," he said. "We manage very well as we are."

Chloe stopped sobbing and hugged him. "You know, I hadn't realized what a nice man you are until now. I took you for granted, and I am very sorry. But I do want to marry Stephanos. I want to marry him very much. If I were a young girl I would say I've fallen in love with him. I am crying because I never thought it would ever ever happen."

Melanthios yelled with delight and hugged her back. "I'll tell him to come and see you, then," he said. "He's waiting downstairs, in the porch outside."

When Stephanos came into the room he seemed to be as tongue-tied as she was. Her heart was beating louder and louder and her face felt burning hot. Eventually he said, "You said yes."

"I …I was very surprised. I never thought…"

"I wasn't sure whether I was imagining it, that you may have felt…"

"But I thought you didn't want to get married again."

"That's what I'd thought too. But when I met you I realized that it wasn't that, exactly."

"What was it?"

"I didn't want to be married to someone who bored me; and so many women do bore me, but you don't, you are different, exciting."

"But how do you know that you won't find me boring too, after you get used to me?"

"No, you don't understand, I am not explaining myself very well. I find you exciting as a person, not just erotically, as I did when I got married the first time; talking to you, seeing you do things, take decisions, you are intelligent, exciting..."

"You said 'not just erotically', does that mean..."

Stephanos took her in his arms and kissed her. And she realized that there were things her body was meant to do and feel that it had never done before.

At about noon that same day Chloe accompanied Mego to the front gate; the Spartan priestess was leaving, and a carriage was waiting to take her to the city, where she would be staying for a few days before returning to Sparta. Chloe hugged Mego and asked, "Are you all right?"

Mego thought about it, and then said, "Yes, actually. I think I am. Coming here, and everything that's happened, it has all helped change my perspective. I mean, things are the same as they were, but I've been able to start to think of what I have actually got, instead of just what I've lost; I have my daughter, I have my husband, my grandchildren and the priesthood." She smiled, and touched Chloe's arm. "I am so happy for you. You deserve some happiness at long last, and the goddess has rewarded you well."

"What do you mean?"

"Think about it. You've given a long and committed service to Artemis Brauronia, the goddess who looks after women and their concerns and their preparation for marriage, and in her

222

sanctuary, at her festival, you met a man you want to marry and who wants to marry you."

"Oh, come on."

"Why not? Don't you think that the gods reward people who serve them well?"

"Yes, sometimes they do. But it's arrogant to think it's happened to you. And why should it?"

"Why not? After all, we know that the gods take an interest in human affairs – sometimes, as you say; and sometimes they go as far as walking among men, disguising themselves, taking a mortal's identity and form, to do things, punish or help certain people."

"In the heroic past they did. But one would have to be insanely arrogant to think it's happened to them. Especially if you are no one special, like me."

"So you think that chance makes better sense."

"I don't know, and just now I don't care. I only want to be happy. I'm scared that it's not going to last."

"Don't worry, it will. Trust me," Mego said, and she put her hand on Chloe's head in an affectionate gesture of farewell. Then she mounted the carriage, which started down the road that snaked between the vineyards, the fig orchards and the olive groves. Chloe stood watching, and just before the carriage disappeared around a curve of the road Mego turned back and waved; as she stood in the blinding sunlight that poured over her from behind, she suddenly looked very tall and shining, like the goddess in the painting in the central suite of the porticoed building. Chloe stared at the retreating figure, and then said to herself aloud, "Nnnaa …it's not possible. Come on, Mego was just joking, or speculating, or maybe even trying to reassure me; it wasn't meant to be a hint!" She laughed and went back into the sanctuary, where Stephanos was waiting by the sacred spring.